GRIEFERS CREEPERS AND SWORDS

Luke and Jamie Reynolds

The front cover was designed by Pixon_designs on fiverr.com

The incredible action scene depiction on the front cover was designed by Trent Savage. You can find him on upwork.com

ISBN: 1973937808

ISBN-13: 978-1973937807

Dedication

I would like to dedicate this book to my son, Luke. You are an incredible gift from God who blesses me every single day! Thank you for always making me proud! I love you always and forever!
Love,
Dad

I also want to dedicate this book to all of my students (past, present, and future). I am so grateful to have the opportunity to teach all of you! I love each and every one of you!

Love,
Mr. Reynolds

Table of Contents

ACKNOWLEDGMENTS

First of all, we would like to thank our Lord and Savior Jesus Christ for giving us the creative ability to write this book. God gave us the gift to create. We are so thankful that we get to use it and share it.

Jamie would like to acknowledge that Luke is the one who actually wrote this book. I typed it and added a few things here or there, but literally 90% of it, came straight from Luke's mind through my fingers to the page.

Luke wants to thank all of his friends at Unity Christian School in Rome, GA: Joe, Bo, Elliott, Sam, Cameron, Landon, Turner, Davis, Moses, and all the rest of Luke's friends have been a source of inspiration for writing this book.

Thank you to Kimberly/Mama for supporting us and giving us helpful ideas, and for being the best Mama and wife in the whole wide world!

Thank you to everyone in our extended families who helped us with launching the website (www.minecraftbooks.us), and who continue to support our efforts. We are so thankful to have such a supporting family!

PREFACE

In this book, you make the choices!! Pick your path wisely!

Start reading on page one, but do not read straight through the book. Instead, follow the directions at the end of each section to choose your path. That's why we call it the "Pick Your Path Series" of books!

If you come to the end of your path, and decide you wish you had made different choices, then feel free to start over or go back to the place where you made a choice you wish you had made differently, and use "The Table of Contents" to help you find your spot.

Above all, HAVE FUN!!!

To see the journey of how the book was *created,* go to our website at www.minecraftbooks.us where you can find Youtube videos, blogs, and other cool things.

WHERE AM I?

You begin to wake up. As you awaken, you realize you are in a beautiful green forest with a very populated village nearby. You begin to think about whether you want to go toward the village or go in the forest instead.

TO GO IN THE FOREST, CONTINUE READING
TO GO TO THE VILLAGE TURN TO PAGE 6

You decide that you would rather go into the forest. It is so green and inviting. You decide you want to stay here for a while, which means you will need to collect wood and build a house. You start to think about what kind of house you want to build. You decide to narrow the choices down to a normal house or a farm house.

TO BUILD A NORMAL HOUSE, CONTINUE READING.
TO BUILD A FARMHOUSE, TURN TO PAGE 4.

You decide to build a normal house. You gather wood, layer it up from its foundation and build your house. The wood planks are not decorative but you do want to have a bed inside. So you go outside the house, wandering around looking for Mary's little lamb. Luckily, you don't have to go far because Mary apparently lost a whole flock of lambs close to where you are building your house. They are just wandering around aimlessly. You take down a couple sheep, gather their wool, and head back to the house.

Arriving back at the house, you craft your bed. Then you put a door on the house. You begin to think about how awesome this house is eventually going to be because you like to dream like that. But, for tonight, it will just be a shelter from the mobs as you are too hot and sweaty to continue working, and nightfall has arrived.

You curl up in your bed and think about how grateful you are that you will be safe from the mobs....at least for tonight.....

Morning comes and you awake and realize you have no tools. Without tools, you won't survive. You go looking for tools. As you wander along thinking about how nice it would be to have a bowl of Fruity Pebbles for breakfast instead of destroying chickens, you come to a hill and begin to go up it until BAM!!! Spiders come jumping out at you!! Your fear turns into relief when you remember spiders don't hurt you in the morning. But, still! Spiders in the morning? Couldn't the forest have waited until later in the day? You begin thinking you might should have gone to the village instead. As you continue walking you remember that if you see spiders at night, it will be a real fight, and somebody will die!

You begin to collect wood when you see something absurd: a burning zombie!! He comes at you with fire in his eyes and a strong desire to turn you into a roasted marshmallow!! Without any weapons, your chances of surviving his evil intentions are less than slim! In fact, your chances are not even chances! They are naïve hopes that have led to the death of many a noob. So you turn around and run as fast as a kid going out to the playground at recess, only you have fear in your heart instead of joy! You run until your lungs burn and you are positive the zombie could never catch you!

As you slow down to a walk, you are thankful that you survived your first zombie scare, and notice a village on the horizon.

You slowly walk in the direction of the village, watching carefully for anything that might harm you. You have already had more surprises of dangerous proportions than you were hoping to find. The last thing you need now is for something else dangerous to come at you before you can get to the village.

Civilization is on the horizon. You finally get to the outer edge of the village.

TURN TO PAGE 6, "THE VILLAGE"

A FARMHOUSE

You decide to build a farm house. Trying not to bite off more than you can chew, you build a beginner farmhouse with a medium sized field of wheat behind the house. You make the field medium sized because you know that if you make it too big you will trample it and the wheat will be as useless as red stone without an iron door.

The inside of your farmhouse has a wooden floor, a small bedroom, and a kitchen. You go out to collect some wheat hoping that you will have enough to fill up your hunger bars. You walk out cautiously, knowing that dangerous mobs could be lurking nearby. Suddenly you see a light green body and you know automatically that it is the body of a creeper!! A chill runs straight up your spine! You run as fast as the wind, fling the door open, slam it shut with all your might, and run to the back of the house! You tumble onto the ground as a hissing sound behind you has you realizing the creeper exploded and messed up all the hard work you put in on the farm house.

You are full of fear because now you know that your life could be in jeopardy since you have no shelter; yet, at the same time you know beyond the shadow of a doubt you are not leaving that wheat field. It is your one hope at survival.

So you decide to craft hay bales, and use them as make-shift walls to replace the farmhouse walls that were damaged. You pray that you will get through the night without creepers attacking you. You knew the walls would break down sooner or later, but had no idea just how soon sooner would be.

But you quickly and suddenly realize sooner is NOW when a swarm of zombies breaks down the hay bales. You realize this is the end. Time stands still for what feels like minutes but passes as seconds as you contemplate the mistake you made by not going to the village.

But, out of nowhere, a blinding light attacks the zombies, and cuts them in half! "*WHAT JUST HAPPENED*?" is all you can think. The next moment has you quickly looking around to find out who your life saving hero is. But you can't see around the room because a zombie's head flies into your face and blocks your view, and you are knocked to the ground!!! Slowly you stand up, gather yourself, and look up to see who saved you. But before you can even get more than a glimpse of who it is, they are gone.

So you get up and are thankful you are still alive. You decide to get out of the area before something else bad happens. You walk along and see that the sun is coming up. You keep walking until you see a village on the horizon.

TURN TO PAGE 6, "THE VILLAGE"

THE VILLAGE

You decide to go into the village. You look around and see lots of villagers, all with many different jobs. One walks up to you and says, “My name is John. I am a carpenter.”

TO KEEP TALKING TO JOHN, KEEP READING

TO TALK TO SOMEONE ELSE TURN TO PAGE 9

John says, “I’ll trade you some tools for some emeralds.”

You tell him, “I don’t have any tools.”

John replies, “The priest over there trades wheat for emeralds.”

You ask the villagers if you can stay in one of their houses for the night.

John replies, “If it’s okay with the mayor, it’s okay with me!” John thinks to himself that he can hardly believe that you came to the village with nothing, and he is amazed that you are without anything to trade.

Hoping to rely on the mercy of others, you wander sheepishly through the village on the lookout for the mayor, and wondering in the back of your mind if you will have a place to lay your head and be safe from the mobs tonight.

Thinking hard about what the mayor might look like, the thought slowly but surely and strongly comes over you that you will not even know if the villager you see is the mayor or not.

So you decide to ask a passerby if they know where the mayor lives. But, at the same time, you don’t want to waste your time with someone who looks unapproachable or like they have no clue what a mayor is.

A man comes walking the opposite direction of you and is wearing a white apron and a Kevlar cloak. Realizing he probably works in the food department of the village, you take to the notion that he might be the answer to your longings to find the mayor, so you decide to approach him gently, and you say softly, "Excuse me sir, my name is Steve. I am hoping to find the mayor of the village. Do you know where he might be or where he lives?"

The man grunts, "What?" And within an instant, you realize you should have let him walk right on by.

But now that you have stopped him, it would be rude to not repeat what you said, so you ask again, this time a little more forcefully, "My name is Steve. I am hoping to find the mayor of the village. Do you know where he might be or lives?"

The man looks at you with a sense of sarcasm oozing out of his eyes, and grunts, "NO! But I know steak is delicious!"

Refusing to give up, and holding on to hope with clinched fists, you ask him, "Do you know someone who *does* know the mayor or where he lives?"

With his husky voice and a lot less sarcasm, he offers, "The librarian might know. The library is right there," as he points to a green and brown building.

A sense of hope and relief perks your mind up a bit and you walk over to the library. You storm in, and in a louder voice than you had planned to use, you say, "Do you know where the mayor is?"

Looking highly offended, the librarian puts her finger over her mouth and says, "SHHHH! Library voices, please," and sits you down with a children's book.

You protest, "What am I supposed to do with this?"

Without hesitation, and in her best Mommy voice, she snaps, "Read it, of course!"

You utter under your breath, "You were no help at all!"

She says, "What was that, sonny?"

"Nothing," you say, as you realize that going in this library was as useless as finding diamonds without having a pick axe.

You hang your head low and exit the library, wondering if the mobs will attack you tonight. You remember fearfully how your friend couldn't find a way to get shelter before the sun went down, and they found his items laying on the ground in a remote location, and never found him.

You begin to walk around in the village again, and you run into a farmer and introduce yourself.

"Hi! My name is Steve! I am looking for the mayor. Do you have any idea where I can find him?"

The farmer speaks quickly and in short bursts, and says, "Yes, I do…Yes, I do…his house is on top of the mountain right over there." The farmer points to a mountain in the distance.

You say, "Come again? What was that?"

The farmer says, "That mountain right over there…his house is up there."

"Oh okay, thank you", you say as you head in the direction that will save your life.

As you get to the base of the mountain, night fall descends on you and you realize that tonight might be your last; but, at the same time hope is filling you up inside knowing that at the top of the mountain, the mayor holds the key to your survival.

And just as you thought your path to that survival was clear, you come to a fork in the path. Although they both head toward the mayor's house, it is clear as the noon day sun that you will have to choose which path to take.

You stop to think it over knowing that this decision could mean life or death. As you begin to weigh the options in your mind, you gaze over your shoulder and realize your choice will be a hasty one because a pack of vacant zombies is coming at you with their arms outstretched and ready to infect you and lower your health!! You must quickly decide whether to take the path to the left or to the right.

TO CHOOSE THE LEFT PATH, TURN TO PAGE 81

TO CHOOSE THE RIGHT PATH, TURN TO PAGE 10

TALK TO SOMEONE ELSE

You decide to talk to someone else. This guy you're talking to doesn't seem like the kind of guy who will have the answers you need.

You walk over to a priest instead. You ask him if he knows anywhere you could sleep. He tells you that the mayor lives up on the far hill over there and has a place you could sleep in. He points to a mountain in the distance and you see a big house on top of the mountain.

So you decide to begin your hike to the hill and wander toward it thinking that you need to hurry because nightfall will soon be approaching.

As you get to the base of the mountain, night fall descends on you and you realize that tonight might be your last; but, at the same time hope is filling you up inside knowing that at the top of the mountain, the mayor holds the key to your survival. And just as you think your path to that survival is clear, you come to a fork in the path.

Although both paths head toward the mayor's house, it is clear as the noon day sun that you will have to choose which path to take. You stop to think it over knowing that this decision could mean life or death. As you begin to weigh the options in your mind, you gaze over your shoulder and realize your choice will be a hasty one because a pack of vacant zombies is coming at you with their arms outstretched and ready to infect you and lower your health!! You must quickly decide whether to take the path to the left or to the right!!

TO CHOOSE THE LEFT PATH, TURN TO PAGE 81

TO CHOOSE THE RIGHT PATH, TURN TO PAGE 10

THE RIGHT PATH

You run up the path to the right as fast as a mine cart on red stone rails! But you haven't gone far when you encounter an eerie creeper!

You realize there is only one hope for your survival. You summersault behind the creeper and punch him in the back, sending him flying toward the zombies who blow up!!

You walk over to inspect the damage when you see something very odd, but true: a music disc dropped from the explosion.

You read the title on the disc: "Imagine Dragons: It's Time". You ponder what you could do with the disc. Could you give it to the mayor as a gift in hopes that he will forget about his path being partly destroyed as a result of the explosion?

You walk on cautiously to be certain of no more mob attacks when suddenly, out of nowhere, you see an enderman! You are very careful not to look at it straight in the eyes because if you do, it will teleport straight toward you and will most likely kill you.

You keep moving and run as fast as you can because the enderman is right next to you! Suddenly, three guys in armor jump out of nowhere and destroy the unsuspecting enderman!! The sound of the enderman's demise comes out of its mouth and sends a shiver up your spine!

You are wondering who these men are. But before you can ask them who they are, they quickly tell you to follow them, and head up the mountain.

The men lead you to the mayor's house where you see a guy who looks like George Washington with a big beard. You think, "*This must be the mayor*!"

In an official voice, he says, "Greetings sir, my name is Lloyd. I am the mayor. What brings you here?"

Feeling overwhelmed and hopeful all at the same time, you utter, "Well, I was coming up here by myself, but these guys in armor led me up here."

The mayor says, "Those are my soldiers, Matt, Scott, and Peter. They are here to protect me from harm. When someone comes up the path, they are putting their safety at risk."

You say, "I understand, sir. I don't mean you any harm or trouble. I am just hoping to find shelter for the night to stay safe from mobs."

The mayor responds, "I see. Well, our house is full, but if you don't mind staying in the outhouse, you are welcome to stay there for tonight. But in the morning you must go."

You begin to think about how your life has become unmanageable. You are now subject to the mercy of a mayor who will not even share his home for *one night*? He has to put me in the *outhouse*?

Well, beggars can't be choosers, I guess, you think to yourself. And you go to the outhouse, having no idea what to expect. You have a very foggy memory of your fifth grade teacher talking about outhouses during history at school, but you do not recall exactly what an outhouse is.

As you enter the dark shed, a nasty smell fills the air, and you realize what an outhouse really is: a shed outside where people use the bathroom. You know you will not sleep well, if at all tonight; but, you also realize that your life has been spared for one more night.

You toss and turn through the first part of the night, and just as you get comfortable enough to really fall asleep a royally dressed woman wakes you up.

Her eyes have circles around them. She says in a serious voice, "You are in grave danger."

Feeling edgy and grumpy, you snap back at her, "You're the one in trouble! You may have forgotten to cross your t's, but your eyes are both dotted!"

She replies eerily, “Is that some kind of teacher pun? And don’t judge me about my eyes, okay? I’m trying to save your life, Mr. Ungrateful!”

You immediately feel guilty and tell her, “I’m sorry for being a jerk, but trying to sleep in this outhouse has made me really grumpy.”

She says, “I have had that feeling too. I’ve had to sleep here too. But you need to come with me, sleepy head, even if I have to drag you.“

You’re not too sure about this! Going along with someone you just met doesn’t seem like a smart thing, but she grabs you by the leg and drags you saying, “Okay, well just lay there then! But I’m going to help you, one way or the other!” She drags you a long way as you ponder the thought of hopping up and smacking her; but, instead you play the role of the lazy minecrafter and let her have her way as she drags you out into an area where nothing can be seen anywhere around you except leaves and trees.

With a contented look and a huffing and puffing voice, she says, “There,” as she drops you. “Now you are in a safe place.”

You cannot believe what just happened! You are not sure if you should be amazed, angry, or confused, but you resign yourself to jabbing a smart comment at her: “What are you? Einstein without his brain and Beast Boy combined?”

She snaps back, “No dummy! And that was a terrible description!” She pulls back some leaves to reveal a ladder.

“Oh wow,” you say, “A ladder! So impressive!” Sarcasm oozes through your body as you try to forget the scrapes on your back caused by being dragged to this useless spot.

She replies, “I’m better than you! You don’t even have a house! And do you think this ladder leads anywhere, or do you think it’s just a ladder?”

You say, “I don’t know! Maybe it leads to a giant statue of your terrible looking face!”

She rolls her circled eyes in annoyance, and says, "Remind me again why I even rescued you?"

As the sun begins to peek over the horizon, she looks down at the ground and her look of sweet irritation turns to bitter resentment as she points toward 2 big chunky dudes running straight at you, and yells, "OH YEAH!! THAT is why I brought you out here! SORRY SUCKER!!!"

You lose sight of her as your attention turns toward defending yourself against the big chunky dudes who are coming at you like grizzly bears charging downhill toward their prey.

One of them grabs you and holds you tight and you know there is no escape. The other big chunky dude plays with you like a toddler bangs a Playskool toy, bringing back memories of your childhood when you used to do the same with your toys.

You realize there is only one hope, albeit a very stupid hope: you try to spin yourself around from his grasp. As you twist your body, you unexpectedly pass gas and his hand loosens slightly, just enough for you to make your escape.

You run as far and as fast as you can until you pass everything you had already encountered in your world. You are panting so hard that you don't see the cactus in front of you and it pricks you in the leg. You cry out in pain a little too loud, because two soldiers, each armed with a diamond sword come out from behind the trees.

Each of the soldiers has "G E " written on their helmet with an ender eye above the letters. You almost jump out of your skin as you realize you are in immediate danger! You look around for shelter or a hiding spot because you know the desert has temples all over it.

You sprint as fast as you can, dodging cactuses along the way until you find a desert temple that has three floors, one on the top, and two below the ground! You dive inside, hoping not to set off any booby traps! You know that somehow you have to hide because the soldiers are hot on your trail.

There is a blue and orange pattern of wool on the ground. You are not sure which one is safe and which one is not (#superstitious). In the middle of the pattern, you see a blue piece of wool just behind a wall.

Being superstitious, you choose the blue square instead of the orange square because you think it is the right choice for survival. You leap to the square to hide and find out you are completely wrong!!

The floor falls out from under you, and you fall into another room! The room has four beige chests. As you hear the soldiers up above you stomping around to find you, anxious hope comes over you as you realize one of the chests might have something to get you out of this mess, and you decide to open one of them.

TO CHOOSE CHEST #1, TURN TO PAGE 15

TO CHOOSE CHEST #2, TURN TO PAGE 16

TO CHOOSE CHEST #3, TURN TO PAGE 78

TO CHOOSE CHEST #4, TURN TO PAGE 80

CHEST ONE

You decide to go with chest one, and rip it open!! Immediately the floor falls out from under you and you are in complete darkness! You look around in hopes that the darkness will turn to light. A tiny sliver of light comes through the walls to shine on the thing you needed least and feared the most: a pack of zombies with a creeper to top it off (like the cherry on the ice cream at Brewster's)!

They all come charging toward you like a pack of coyotes attacking a wounded rabbit! You realize this is your end. The creeper explodes right next to you, which you thought would be the last of you, sending you flying farther into the darkness, and you are left with half a health bar. You can barely see the pack of zombies that were coming at you, but you feel like you have a sliver of a chance at survival until you turn around to run and BAM!!! A ZOMBIE WHO CAME UP BEHIND YOU FINISHES YOU OFF!!! LIGHTS OUT FOR YOU!!!

The End

CHEST TWO

You quickly open chest #2 to see sand and dirt! You realize the sand and dirt will be very helpful, if you can just find a use for them. You think about how to use them, but just before a great idea comes to you, one of the soldiers falls through the hole above you and grabs you, nabbing your inventory. The other soldier uses the dirt and sand to make a staircase up to the top of the desert temple. Once you are at the top, they decide to take you somewhere. But you have no idea where you are going.

TURN TO PAGE 17

THE SOLDIERS

More than a little anxious, you try to resist the soldiers taking you with them, and they trip you, and begin dragging you. They drag you for what feels like miles and miles. Then they start pulling on your shirt.

"Watch the shirt," you yell. "This is the only one I have!"

The soldiers tell you that if you want to live, you will be quiet right now. Unwilling to risk your life over a shirt, you keep quiet but are so angry that you wonder if there is steam coming out of your ears, like Popeye before eating a can of spinach. You are in no shape to pull off anything that Popeye can do with his strength. You are growing weaker by the minute and wonder when this horrible nightmare will end when you see a gigantic gold and light blue palace up ahead.

The soldiers go to the gates where there is a sophisticated looking redstone identification device, which asks for the soldiers' identification. One of the soldiers says, "Delta 2297." The other soldier says, "Bravo 2461."

The computer opens the doors to the palace, and all at once you are surrounded by colorful pictures and servants dressed in colorful outfits.

You see a squad of troopers just like the ones who are carrying you. As you pass other soldiers, you find it very strange that none of the soldiers talk to each other. You think about how cold hearted these guys are and a sick feeling takes you over.

You go a long distance through the palace until finally, you come to a staircase. The soldiers take you down the staircase.

You think to yourself, *this part must be the not so colorful part of the palace.* All you can see is gray and black, like an old black and white movie. The guards keep taking you farther until you reach a door. They open the door, which leads to a different part of the palace, full of color like the first section of the palace you already went through. The soldiers push you down, and you fall into a kneeling position.

You hope with yearning that you have never felt before that the soldiers will leave you there, but, instead they hover above you. At the front of the room are two huge golden chairs with a person wearing a black hood sitting in each of them. You think to yourself that they must be the king and queen.

The queen speaks in a sly voice: “Hello, Steve.”

“Who are you? And how do you know my name?” you shout back.

She replies in a royal voice, “Oh, I know everything.” As she takes off her hood, you know you will never forget her face, a face that only a mother could love. The sick feelings you have welling up inside you only get worse.

“You are at a crossroads, Steve,” says the evil queen. “You are now under the full control of the Griefer Empire. I am going to give you a decision: you may become one of us or you may die.”

“Wow! What a choice, my queen! Do I get to become the prince or is that spot reserved for one of the big chunky dudes who tried to turn me into a pile of remains for the vultures?”

“No, you dummy! You’re being sarcastic toward me when you could already be dead?” she replies.

“Sarcasm is my spiritual gift, my queen,” you say bluntly.

“So what do you want to do then, Steve? Do you want to turn evil or would you rather die?” says the girl as she gives you a deadly look.

TO TURN EVIL, TURN TO PAGE 20

TO DIE, TURN TO PAGE 19

NEVER SAY DIE

"I'd rather die than turn evil," you tell the queen as you grit your teeth.

"Okey dokey then, Mr Noob King. Your wish is my command," the queen snaps back quickly.

The queen snaps her fingers sharply. One of her body guards gets up, and pushes you into a hole, also known as your death.

As you fall out of the world, you think about how you could have been so prosperous being evil. But because things did not work out that way, it looks like it's curtains for you.....unless of course, you want to change your mind, turn evil, and turn to page 20....(there's always a chance you can become good again)

TURN EVIL

You decide that if death or turning evil are your only two options, then turning evil is really your *only* choice. So you tell the girl, “I do not want to turn evil, but I do not want to die either. So, I am surrendering my will and joining the evil side.”

She tells you that her name is Megan, and she is one of the leaders of The Griefer Empire, and now that you are one of them, you will need to follow orders at all times or you will not like what happens to you.

Then Megan says, “First, you are going to change the way you look. Right now, you look like a wamby pamby, bland-faced cream puff. I want you to look tough! People need to be scared of you!” She hands you a suit of chrome armor that shines brightly in the sun and tells you to put it on. Then she gives you a helmet to match the suit and orders you to put the helmet on and stand up straight at attention.

You think to yourself that your choice to go down this evil path has taken away your ability to choose, even right down to what you are wearing. As far as you are concerned, you look like a sorry excuse for an old-school silver lunch box!

“You are soldier number 777! Do you understand that? You do not have a name anymore! You are now simply called soldier 777,” the queen yells at you.

You manage to grumble that you understand without lashing out at Megan, which is what you really want to do. But you know that lashing out could mean death, because other soldiers are nearby.

Megan says, “Your first job is to go out and capture a man named Ethan. He has been playing games and tricking us for years, and now it is time for his fun to stop! It is not a game anymore! It has not been a game for a long time. He just doesn’t realize it. So here’s a sword, a bow, and some arrows. You will need to travel to the other side of the mountain to find his village. On the other side of the mountain, there is a giant red farmhouse right next to a stream. Go to that farmhouse, and you will meet up with 2 other soldiers who will go on the mission with you."

You grab the weapons she hands you, put them in your inventory, and get moving quickly so you can make it to the farmhouse before dark.

As you walk along at a fast pace, you begin to think about how your life has taken a turn that you did not expect at all. You have never been an evil person, and you are not comfortable with the idea of capturing Ethan; however, you do have to admit that the feeling of power that may come from working on the evil side seems like something cool, a way to take control of things before they take control of you. You go back and forth in your mind between good and evil thoughts until you get to the base of the mountain.

At the base of the mountain, you find a cow walking along the edge of the land where the forest meets the grass. You think to yourself that your hunger bars are rather low, and that it would not hurt to have a meal. You take out your bow and arrow, and aim for the cow.

As you release the arrow, you think about how cool it would be to live in a future world where you could go to a place where lots of people go to eat food that someone else killed and prepared. If you could name it, you would call it Longhorn Steakhouse. That would be so yummy! But for now, it is time to finish off this cow! You shoot it with another arrow! It runs toward you, and you finish it off with your diamond sword!

"*Where is my pick axe when I need it?*" you think to yourself as you think about mining the stone for a furnace. You walk around for a while looking for stone and eventually see some. You take out your diamond sword, and start mining the stone. But now you are going to have to make a crafting table to craft the furnace.

"Man, I wish they would invent gas grills!" you shout. But,

until then, it's time to fetch some wood to get the crafting table made.

Being the smart Minecrafter you are, you killed a cow right where the woods meet the grass and there are plenty of trees right next to you. Taking down trees is one of your less favorite things to do in Minecraft, but it sure is good exercise. Yes, indeed! The sweat running all over you tells you it is almost dinner time. As you finish driving splinters into your fists by getting wood, your stomach growls a long growl and you continue to work until you complete the crafting table. You throw on the stone you mined, and craft it into a furnace. You place the furnace down, place the meat in it, and throw some logs on the furnace to get it cooking.

When the process is finished, you take out two pieces of meat, and scarf them down like King Kong, putting pieces in each hand.

As you finish, you see a glimpse of the village you are supposed to go to in the distance. You decide to mine your crafting table and your furnace to take it with you. *Looks like it's on the road again*, you think to yourself!

You walk into the forest, feeling a little bit uneasy because mobs can spawn under shady trees.

Suddenly an arrow hits you in the shoulder! You yelp in pain but stop yourself to try to find who shot you! You gaze around quickly to see a skeleton under a tree!

You charge at the skeleton with your sword drawn, and slam your sword into the skeleton with all your might! He turns into a ball of smoke and drops a bone and an arrow! You pick both items up and put them into your inventory. You are very pleased with this find! But then on the other hand, you do not want to interfere with any more mobs.

So you run through the forest as fast as you can until you reach the village!

As you approach the village, you see two soldiers standing on the village road. One of them is slamming an axe into a tree while the other swings his sword into the air.

You go over to them and ask, "Are you the soldiers I'm supposed to meet up with?"

They say in unison, "State your name!"

"I'm soldier 777," you say plainly.

"Yep you're the one! I'm soldier 877 and this is soldier 321! Let's go find Ethan," one of the soldiers replies.

You look around for the location Megan told you about. You spot the red barn as quick as a hawk finds its food.

"Let's go guys," you shout as you point in the direction of the barn.

"Who made you the leader," says soldier 321 as he pushes you out of the way.

You are not really sure what the big deal is but you are sure this guy means business, so you let him get ahead of you but then try to regain the lead the whole way to the barn. You get close to catching him and start hand fighting for first position until soldier 877 yells, "Break it up, you two!"

The two of you both pause and soldier 877 says, "How about this? Soldier 777 can make our battle plan, and soldier 321 can lead us in combat. How does that sound?"

"Fine," you say angrily. Soldier 321 agrees angrily as well.

For the rest of the walk you plan out the battle. Soldier 877 will be at the top of the farmhouse entrance. You and soldier 321 will be at the back with your bow and arrows ready, so that no matter which way Ethan tries to run, he will be blocked. Finally, you reach your destination and approach cautiously.

You whisper the plan to the other two soldiers. They agree and all of you stand at your positions. You wait as patiently as you can for Ethan to open the door.

Suddenly, the door opens toward soldier 877, who clobbers Ethan with his diamond sword, leaving Ethan with half a heart!

"Remember," you shout, "Our orders are to capture him, not to destroy him!"

"How about this," says soldier 321, "Soldier 877, makes sure Ethan won't get away while soldier 777 and I loot Ethan's house?"

With every wrong thing you're doing, you feel your stomach getting sicker. You walk into the house with soldier 321. You instantly see a chest in the living room. You run over to it and open it. It has leather armor labeled "pajamas", a bucket of milk, and a cookie labeled "midnight snack". You take them, thinking they will be somewhat useful.

Soldier 321 shouts, "Over here!" He shows you a chest in what looks like an armory with tons of armor stands with seemingly every kind of armor in Minecraft. Absolutely amazing!

You take some diamond armor, put it in your inventory, and then open a chest at the end of the room. You open the chest to find a stack of enchanted golden apples and two diamond pick axes! You split the golden apples with soldier 321, give one diamond pick axe to soldier 321 and keep one pick axe for yourself.

Then you see two rooms: one you love, because it's the kitchen, the other you're not too sure about because you can't see what is in it.

TO GO INTO THE KITCHEN, TURN TO PAGE 25

TO GO INTO THE ROOM YOU CAN'T SEE IN, TURN TO PAGE 26

THE KITCHEN

Being that you love kitchens, you decide to shrug off any thoughts of what might be in the unknown room, and head straight for the kitchen. As you walk into the room, you see 2 chests: one labeled "dessert", the other labeled "delicious dinner". You decide to open both chests. Inside the "delicious dinner chest", there are baked potatoes, steak, cooked pork chops, stew, watermelon (God's gift to Minecrafters), carrots, golden carrots, and mutton chops. There is so much food that you do not want to be greedy, and you leave some of it behind for the other two soldiers, and start off this buffet of mass consumption with eating 3 bowls of mushroom stew, refilling your hunger bars plentifully.

Dessert time! You rip open the "dessert chest" and find a stack of cookies, pumpkin pie, and cake. You decide to eat one of each.

After eating a cookie, pumpkin pie, and cake, you feel like a kid who refused to eat anything except sweets. But, oh well, you're on the evil side. With a gut full of goodness, you feel your looting is finished and you head back outside to meet up with soldier 321 and soldier 877 who are standing together with Ethan.

TURN TO PAGE 30, "THE SOLDIERS AND ETHAN"

THE ROOM YOU CAN'T SEE IN

You decide to take a chance and go into the room you can't see in. You nervously walk toward the room's closed door. You grab the doorknob as your hand shakes a bit. You turn the knob slowly, push open the door even more slowly: ....CREEEAAK.....as the door opens you can hardly believe your eyes!!

There are tons of armored suits just like the armor you have on! But then you see what you did NOT want to see: 2 diamond golems from the "Golem World Mod"! Oh NO! What are you going to do now? You have to make a split second decision:

TO FIGHT, TURN TO PAGE 27

TO RUN, TURN TO PAGE 29

YOU FIGHT

You are not about to back down from these villager protectors!! One of them swings his long blue arms at you, but you dodge his blow! You slide under his legs and use your diamond sword to knock him into the wall so hard that he forgets who his Mom is and loses half his health!

You then change tactics to take out the second golem! You quickly whip out your bow and arrow, and shove arrows into the bow, one after the other, shooting them just as fast as you can get them loaded! Since golems are extremely slow, they cannot hit you while you're firing the arrows.

But you almost forgot about the first golem, and he clobbers you over the head with a swift smack of his bold blue arm! Your health goes down more than half way! You are not sure you made the right choice to stay and fight. Is this going to be it? Is this the end?

He swings to deliver another blow and you see it coming right toward your head, but JUMP! You jump back just in the nick of time and dodge his death strike! (#Progamingskills)

Suddenly, an idea bursts into your brain like fireworks on the 4th of July: you felt like Max from Shark Boy and Lava Girl! Your idea is that golems are hostile against each other, not just their enemies! If you could get them to notice each other, you could get them to destroy each other! You could get behind them and swing your sword into them, and they would fall on each other like dominos! Time to carry out the plan before the golems own you!

You run as fast as you can behind a golem! You slam your sword into his diamond body! With all the knock-back power of the sword, he falls back on to the other golem! The two golem's eyes meet, and it is on like Donkey Kong! Now it's time to sit back and enjoy this mob battle, just like on Youtube! You wish for popcorn and soda as the two of them exchange blows, and a grin bigger than that of Bozo the clown crosses your face.

One of the golems finally gets destroyed by the other, leaving the sad and unhealthy remaining golem who just needs to be put out of his miserable one health bar misery. And so you figure the most humane way to do that is to get out your bow and arrow, aim carefully, and drop him like a sack of taters. Being the humane Minecrafter you are, you do just that, and the last golem disappears, leaving behind 3 diamonds, which you happily snap up and throw into your inventory. You then grab the other 3 diamonds from the other golem that got destroyed and you feel like a champ!

"*I think I've had enough looting for today*," you think to yourself, and you head back out to try to meet up with the other soldiers who hopefully have Ethan with them.

As you get outside, you see soldier 877, soldier 321, and Ethan all standing together. You walk up to talk to them.

TURN TO PAGE 30, "THE SOLDIERS AND ETHAN"

RUN FOR YOUR LIFE!

Rather than risk getting killed by those crazy looking diamond golems that swing their arms like monkeys trying to beat up a heavy weight champ, you decide to end your looting early, and bolt out of the room like you were playing Temple Run and the monkey was the golems! But as you turn a corner you realize the diamond golems are coming after you! They are really slow but you feel like this may not end well.

You whip out your bow and arrow to take aim, but as you start to aim, soldier 321 jumps out of a room right in front of the golems and corners both of the golems! And it begins! A lashing like you have never seen!

Even with only a 7 damage sword against 2 100 health beasts, he plunges his sword so quickly and aggressively that the golems are destroyed in no time at all!

You now have a new found respect for the fighting skills of soldier 321! Wow! What a show! You yell at him, "Nice job, soldier! Thanks for the help!"

Soldier 321 looks up at you with deadly seriousness and says, "You don't have to be so disrespectful about it newbie!"

"Disrespectful? I was just patting you on the back sincerely," you reply.

Soldier 321 looks you straight in the eye and says, "If you do it again, I'll slam you with my fist!"

"Make way for Mr. Intensity," you think to yourself. But anyway, the way you look at it, you are stuck with these guys. The two of you head out to meet up with soldier 877 and Ethan. As you get outside, you see both of them and all of you stand together to talk.

TURN TO PAGE 30, "THE SOLDIERS AND ETHAN"

THE SOLDIERS AND ETHAN

Soldier 877 takes out a map from his inventory and shows you the place where you will camp for the night: an open area next to a forest. "It won't be too far away!" says soldier 877.

You say, "Well, time to go!" And the four of you head toward the area, which is just an hour away. You assign jobs to the soldiers. Soldier 321 will guard Ethan. Soldier 877 will lead them to the destination. And you will attack any mobs foolish enough to attack the group.

You walk and walk until finally, soldier 877, says you are half way there. When you reach your destination, you see a cave nearby.

You decide to be cautious because you know mobs spawn in dark places like caves; still, your curiousness about what kind of ores will be in the cave is too great to keep you from looking inside.

You enter the cave slowly and cautiously. But as soon as you do, a cave spider pounces on your face and bites you, weakening you with poison and your health declines to half a heart! You fall on the ground in pain! As soon as you do, two zombies come lumbering out of the cave!

But, soldier 321, like your knight in shining armor, comes to your rescue, and skillfully slays all the mobs, and gives you a bucket of milk to help wear off the poison effect.

He yells at you, "You've got to learn a sense of self-defense! Meet me tonight when the rest are asleep, and I will show you!"

Thinking that his idea of meeting secretly at night is pretty random, you hesitate, but then reply "Okay". Note to reader: you know what is coming on if you have ever watched a movie. You pick yourself up and walk to the campsite.

Soldier 877 gives the orders this time, and you were not going to argue because you do not want to make soldier 321 mad.

Soldier 877 tells soldier 321 to go get wood. When soldier

877 finishes chopping down wood, he gives the wood to you so you can make a temporary house, that all important survival shack that every Minecrafter needs when night comes.

While soldier 321 is chopping down wood, you will be guarding Ethan. And soldier 877 will be looking for food.

Soldier 877 hands you some lead and a fence to tie Ethan up. You sit with your eyes on full alert, staring at Ethan. You sit there until you finally get bored. You start swinging your sword off into the distance, aiming your bow and arrow at nearby trees.

Finally, after what seems like a year, soldier 321 comes to meet you, and gives you the supplies needed to build your temporary shelter. Being the pro builder you are, you get it done in one hour, furnace, crafting table and all. And that is just enough time for soldier 877 to come back with some steak, pork chops, and beef....and, of course some rotten flesh for prisoner Ethan.

You all sit down in the cozy little shelter. Finally, after finishing the food, you are stuffed. Soldier 877 commands you to put the rotten flesh down for Ethan. Ethan eats the rotten flesh very slowly. Apparently he knows that rotten flesh sometimes makes you hungrier.

You are not so ready for whatever soldier 321 has planned for you tonight. You are already pretty sleepy, but decide to wait for soldier 321 outside and force your eyes to stay open. When soldier 321 comes out with his sword drawn and a quiver on his back, he looks like a savage. With a firm and low voice, he tells you to follow him.

Soldier 321 sprints into the forest. You follow him, huffing and puffing like the big bad wolf did after trying to blow the brick house in. Finally, you reach a clearing in the forest. Soldier 321 is standing there along with targets made out of wool and armor stands that look like dummy targets for practicing on.

Soldier 321 tells you, “I am going to tell you one of the most important things you need to know in Minecraft: whenever you enter a dark area, have your sword drawn! Expect the unexpected! Mobs are relentless against Minecrafters! Never let any mushy, emotional feelings out. It lowers your combat skills.

You think to yourself, *"Is this the Batman of Minecraft I am talking to?"*

Soldier 321 shows you a legendary sword technique on a dummy, throwing his sword up in the air, and watching it lunge down into the dummy, hitting it full throttle. Soldier 321 takes the sword out and slams it into the dummy again as hard as possible, destroying the dummy in one strike!

"Now it's your turn" he says, looking at you with a look of high expectation. You run at a dummy with all your speed and swing your sword straight down the middle of the dummy! The dummy cracks in half! But you still had to destroy the two remaining pieces. With two brisk hits of your sword, the dummy's remains shatter to pieces!

"Good, but needs improvement," says soldier 321.

"Good!? That's all I get?" you question in protest.

He ignores your comment and says, "Now it's time for arrow training! You get three shots!" He takes out an arrow, aims, and hammers home a bullseye. He uses the other two arrows to do exactly the same. "Your turn, " he says, more forcefully than before.

You take out your bow and arrow, aim carefully, and nail the bullseye! "Wahoo!" you shout.

"Remember what I told you about keeping your feelings in," says soldier 321.

In a terrible impression of a brooding voice, you say, "Okay."

Soldier 321 slams his head against his hand and says, "We've got a lot of work ahead of us."

Suddenly you see Ethan running through the forest! *What in the world!? What happened?!* "It's Ethan!!!" you shout.

"Let's take him down!" yells soldier 321. You both take out your bow and arrows, load, pull back, aim, and even with a moving target, you connect, and knock Ethan to the ground! You rush over and tie his hands with lead!

Trying to be unemotional like soldier 321 told you to be, you say plainly, "Come with me, and you will not die." You hurry to the shack, not wanting to risk another escape. This time you put Ethan in the bedroom of the shack, take his inventory, and put him in iron bars. Then you lay down in your bed and catch some zzzz's.

You wake up with that feeling of, "OH yeah! I'm the king of the village, people!" Then you remember your boss Megan. Oops, forgot about her. Yikes. You walk over to see if the other soldiers are still in bed. Nope! They are not in bed. They must be in the main room of the shack. They must be fixing breakfast, and boy are you hungry. You walk in to the kitchen area and they are not there. Where could they be? You walk outside to see what they are up to. Could they be starting a farm or something? It would be pointless because you are moving on today. Hmmm. You scan the area and look as far as you can in the distance for them, and you catch a tiny glimpse of two people with the same armor on that you have on. Yep! That's them, you think.

You run through the forest partly angry, and partly curious. You run up to them and yell, "What are you doing, going out without me knowing?"

"Helping you," they yell back in unison. "Look at that village over there! If you can destroy it, take some loots, and bring back prisoners to Megan you will look really good in her eyes, get points, and rank up! Take this TNT, and flint and steel, and blow that village to pieces!"

Part of you thinks, "Funniest thing ever!!" The other part of you thinks, "Why am I doing this?!" But either way, you are stuck being evil, you decide. So you might as well do it right.

For some reason, the library is the first place that comes to your mind when you think of things to blow up. So you head that way. You walk in the door of the library, place a TNT block down, light it up with flint and steel, and run like a man being chased by hornets! BOOM!!! Your brain shakes in your skull, and you look back to see a mushroom cloud that used to be the library! The only thing left to do now is take the books and take the librarian prisoner.

You march back to the rubble like a good little evil warrior and find the librarian shivering in the only corner left of the library. You run over to her with your diamond sword drawn.

The librarian quickly writes a note and throws it out onto the streets of the village. After writing the note, she screams, "Help!" But you quickly cover her mouth, tie her hands behind her back using lead, and take her back to soldier 877 and soldier 321, thinking that will be the best choice, rather than going all the way back to the cabin.

You pick up all the books laying around what is left of the library, and put them in your inventory. You're not going to have a lot of space left for the rest of the loots, you think to yourself. But you decide to get going toward a new task anyway. It is time for more evil!

But as you walk along in thought about your next act of evil, you look up and there in front of you is an army of village guards. And in front of them all is your worst enemy of all: an iron golem! *"No matter,"* you think!

You make a fire ring around them with your flint and steel, and shoot arrows at the iron golem and village guards one after the other! Finally, all of the village guards go down and the iron golem only has two health bars left! You hit it twice with your arrows and it goes down in a cloud of huffing and smoke! You decide to take only one of the guard's shields because your inventory is almost full. Thanks to the newest version of Minecraft, you could wield both your sword and the village guard's shield!

Time to wreak some more havoc, you think to yourself as you walk around looking for your next victims. How about the blacksmith? He'll have some delicious food for Megan's next meal, and he'll also have a variety of weapons and armor.

You walk in and the old and experienced blacksmith immediately recognizes your armor and quickly yells, "Evacuate!!" He jumps out the back window of the blacksmith shop!

"Oh, no you don't," you shout as you walk up to the window and shoot him in the leg with an arrow, dropping him like a bad habit! You open the chest that is always at the back of a blacksmith's shop, and find: an iron helmet, iron boots, 3 apples, 3 carrots, and a bowl of rabbit stew. What a combination! So this is all this guy has to live on, you think to yourself. What's so bad about going to jail, if this is the way you are having to live? You walk out of the shop and tie the blacksmith's hands with lead. Another victim! Score more points for Megan! As you are tying his hands with lead, he finally says, "They finally got me!"

You shout back to him firmly, "Come quietly grandpa"

He snaps back, "I'm only 95!"

"Whatever you say. I'm just going to bring you back to the other soldiers," you say calmly. And with that, you move him away from the building, lay down some TNT, light it up, and get away! BOOM! That is better than fireworks on the 4th of July!

You bring the blacksmith back to the other soldiers, turn back around to the village, and go back one last time for some more evil fun. You run over to the farm to do some food looting. Let's see, on side one of the farm, you notice as you walk up, there are God's greatest edible gifts to man: watermelons. While on the other side of the farm, you see a pumpkin patch. You think about adding sugar and making pumpkin pie. And if someone gets in your way, they are going to get spooked a whole lot worse than a kid does on Halloween.

No sooner does that thought cross your mind, than you see a farmer walking out into the field. As soon as he sees the "GE" written on top of your helmet, he runs away screaming like a girl who just saw Herobrine! But you stop him in his tracks with your sword! Then you lay the diamond to him! Feeling like you are on an infomercial, you try your best to display to the customers all the things your sword can do. And when you are finished with the farmer, you feel like all the customers want to buy your sword with some emeralds. You are the stuff! And so is your sword!

Now it's time to go back to the palace. You reunite with soldier 321 and soldier 877 and head on your way. On the way to the palace, soldier 321 gives your ego a boost by telling you how impressed he is with all of your captures. Finally you reach the palace. You walk up to the castle gates and two soldiers greet you.

One of them says, "We will take the prisoners to Megan."

"Okay," you say, feeling relieved of the responsibility of having to make sure they don't get away.

Soldier 321 jumps in front of you and yells to the soldiers taking away the prisoners, "What's your soldier number?"

"Soldier 111," one of them eagerly yells.

The other soldier chimes in, "Soldier 615!"

"Go ahead then," says Soldier 321.

You open the door to the palace and decide you want to go along with the soldiers taking your captives to Megan. After all, you want to get credit for capturing them!

Arriving at the palace, you walk in to the throne room, and ask Megan if she is surprised by all your good work.

She replies with a smile and says, "Yes, I am very impressed, indeed. Now you will be ranked up to rank 1! You get your very own quarters with a servant, flaming arrows, and a new enchanted sword! Well done soldier!"

Suddenly, in the background you see the two soldiers tip

toeing out of the palace with the captives who have been set free! You shoot one of the flaming arrows at one of the fugitives. With them caught on fire, you take out your new enchanted sword, and run and charge at them. You manage to slam your sword into your target, but the other soldier winds up hitting you with his own sword! But that was no matter to you. You get back up and jab your sword as hard as you can into the soldier who just hit you! He falls to the ground in pain, which gives you enough time to finish off your original target.

"Finish him slowly and painfully," says Megan.

You think to yourself*, that will be fine with you because you have time to spare.*

You walk with your sword casually over to the fugitive. You throw your sword into the air, jump up, and bicycle kick it down to finish the fugitive off!

"No! Daniel!" shouts the other fugitive. You're going to try a different approach to take out the other soldier. You stand her up, swing your fist around in a circle like Popeye, and finish her with one swift blow! You look around for your "Easy Button" and feel like yelling "AYAYAYAYAY", but do not see an "Easy Button", and for some reason, you decide not to yell.

"Very nice job, soldier! You aren't the newbie I thought you were," says Megan. "At ease, soldier. You may return to visit your quarters," she continues.

Tired and sweaty from battling, you walk to your quarters and open the door. The first thing you see is your servant. You walk over to him and fist bump him, saying, "What up, bro!"

He speaks back in a spiffy voice back to you, "Very good sir."

You then observe the room, and see a small but beautiful kitchen, an intricately designed bedroom with chiseled quartz walls, and a picture of an enderman inside. You then see the biggest part of the whole place: a living room complete with a couch and an indoor fountain.

You decide to walk to the chest because you are very

hungry after your long trip. You take a golden carrot and a cookie from the chest in the kitchen. You start gnawing away on the carrot. You decide to take a nap because wearing out enemies takes its toll after a while, and you have worn out plenty of them.

You quickly fall into a deep sleep, never knowing just how tired you were while visions of Super Mario Maker and Zelda dance in your head. When you wake up, you find yourself face to face with something you didn't see before: a chest with a sign above it that reads "Targets".

You open the chest out of curiosity because you know that you couldn't just put a target in a chest in Minecraft. But when you open the chest, you get what the sign meant. It is a book with fugitives you have to hunt down.

You open the book and flip through the pages. One page says "Collin", and lists all the things he has done wrong with his picture above them. Collin has on a purple and black patterned shirt, and for some reason he is pictured sticking his tongue out. When you see the charges, you understand why. They read "Charges: Taunting a Griefer Empire Guard".

The next page reads, "Ben," and has a picture of a very angry looking man dressed in black. He is charged with sending a Griefer Empire Guard for the hills.

Another page reads, "Lisa". In the picture she is holding a Griefer Empire guard by the neck with her other arm outstretched like she is about to punch him. She is wearing a plaid coat and a Nyan Cat shirt. Under the charges it reads: "Charged with stealing and threatening a Griefer Empire Commander."

You decide to consult with Soldier 321 and Soldier 877 about which of the "Targets" to take down first. You ask your servant where Soldier 877 and Soldier 321's quarters are.

He replies, "Right down the hall, sir."

You walk down the hall and open the door to Soldier 877 and Soldier 321's quarters. You walk into the quarters and find that their quarters are like yours; but, the only difference is they have a training room instead of a living room, and an armor stand with iron armor on it and a noob face on top of it that reads: "Noob Lord".

Soldier 321 is practicing his swordsman skills on the armor stand, chopping it into pieces. Not wanting to get in the way of Soldier 321's rage, you stroll casually past and head to Soldier 877's room.

"'Sup," Soldier 877 blurts as he nods. He is crafting wooden swords and throwing them at a leather armor stand with a zombie face on it. You are impressed with his skills. Holding the pictures of the "targets" in your hand, you hold them up and raise your voice as if to sound tempting and say, "I was just wondering if you want to go take down some of these targets."

Soldier 877 replies quickly, "Of course I want to! I wonder why Megan didn't give us those! Let's go ask William if he wants to come."

"Okay wait! Who is William?!" You are not sure if you heard him right.

"OH!! Must have flipped my wording around," says Soldier 877.

"All right, I know you did that on purpose! What's the real story!"

"Well, the real story is that I spawned into this world just like you guys, and I don't know how it happened. But anyway, I saw this man in the background. I walked closer to him. I looked at his gamer tag, and it read 'William'. He was rolling and tumbling through the trees like a ninja. He finally walked over to me and asked me, 'who are you?' I replied, 'Al'. He said to me, 'I am William. Do you want to be friends?' So we became friends, adventuring from one place to the next, never having a place to settle down, mining, fighting, and exploring. We were the best of the best! But it all ended in a moment when 3 Griefer Empire Guards raided the village we were staying in.

We were spared, brought here, and became soldiers."

Shocked and a little confused, you say, "You guys had this secret all the time, and you never told me? Well, I have a similar story to you, and my real name is Steve." You proceed to tell him your whole story from the beginning.

The two of you walk with Soldier 877 into the training room and somehow Soldier 321 instantly senses that you now know his real name. Maybe it was the look on your face. Maybe it was the look on Soldier 321's face. Maybe he had overheard your conversation. But no matter the reason, Soldier 321 seems a bit excited and has a positive attitude, and says, "Well, now he knows the real story. Now we're a real team!"

You head out the door to tell Megan you are going to slay some fugitives. She approves and you are off on your journey. "Which one should we go for first?" you ask, showing the other guys the target pictures.

You look over the pictures together and Al says, "Let's go for Collin! He looks easy."

"No, I think we should go for Lisa. She's the hardest looking one to catch," Says William.

You interrupt and throw in your two cents: "No! We should go for Ben! He's right in the middle!"

Al blurts out quickly, "Here is why we should go for Collin: he can be like our warm up round. Then we can go to Ben, then Lisa as a boss battle."

William argues back, "Look, if you want to wear your baby gloves to start, you're not a real soldier. Lisa is the toughest and she wears Nyan Cat shirts. How do you beat that?"

Instead of jumping in to argue any more, you just keep your mouth shut and let the two of them talk it out. But as they talk, you know you will have the choice of who to go after first because you are Steve. You are the man. You pick the path. *So put a sock in it boys, I get to decide,* you think to yourself.

IF YOU WANT TO GO AFTER COLLIN FIRST, TURN TO PAGE 47 (TURN PAGE FOR MORE CHOICES)

IF YOU WANT TO GO AFTER BEN FIRST, TURN TO PAGE 42

IF YOU WANT TO GO AFTER LISA FIRST, TURN TO PAGE 44

GO AFTER BEN FIRST

You decide to go find Ben first. “Come on guys! Let’s go find Ben,” you tell William and Al excitedly. They follow after you. You run and run, but then realize it is almost sunset. You make a quick decision to soldier on instead of building a shelter. You find your reward for your perseverance! There are two guards guarding an entrance. These guards have to be guarding something, so you decide to attack them.

Al jumps and hits a soldier right in the head. You charge at one soldier, weakening him significantly. The soldier has the eyes of someone who just got bad news from a doctor. Al finishes him off with a blow to the leg, and the soldier disappears. William finishes off the resisting guard.

You open up the entrance and find a kingdom of jewels. What an incredible sight to behold! You pick your jaw up off the floor and find that there is a wall surrounding the city with guards on the top of the wall. But using your ninja skills, you dart past them without being detected.

Al busts open the gate, and you walk into the city. Out in the vast distance, you spot a small Collinboard next to what looks like a flourishing farm. The Collinboard reads, “Fresh Melons From Ben’s Farm”. You stop in your tracks, and tell the others, “Look guys, it’s Ben’s farm! The guy we’re looking for!”

You walk into the farm only to find that the farm is completely inactive. You could not find Ben or even an employee around. Suddenly, you see a sign stuck in the ground in the middle of the actual property that reads, “This Site Will Be Refurbished and Refined by The GREAT Griefer Empire”.

“Oh, come on! Someone beat us here,” you say. “Ben must be long gone by now.”

You realize that your hunger bars are very low and begin to walk to find a place to eat. Along the way, you see a dirtied up business card on the ground. You pick it up and see that it reads, "The Diamond Deli: moded cakes, pork chops, steak, and all the fixin's". All of you walk slowly to the Diamond Deli, careful not to use your half a hunger bar by sprinting. When you arrive at The Diamond Deli, you open the door, sit down, and find that your server comes over immediately, and quick as lightning, you throw off your armor and tell the others to do the same.

You all take off your armor and put it in your inventories. William is wearing a lava colored Adidas shirt to match his lava colored hair. Al is wearing a shirt that reads. "Bro, just chill" He also has a rainbow Mohawk. You look over the menu and narrow it down to either watermelon or mutton chops. Which do you choose?

TO ORDER WATERMELON, TURN TO PAGE 53

TO ORDER MUTTON CHOPS, TURN TO PAGE 52

GO AFTER LISA FIRST

"Let's go for Lisa first," you say. The others agree.

You rush out of the base eager to catch the rebellious criminal! You run to the far left until you reach a peculiar looking entrance guarded by two guards. They don't look very alert.

All at once, you and William take out your swords ready to do battle. You charge at the guards, taking them by surprise. They take serious damage, but are now extremely alert! William charges at one of the guards but has the breath knocked out of him from a strong counter blow. With that guard focused on William, you stab that guard right in the shoulder. He falls to the ground in pain, but not yet defeated.

You turn around to find the second soldier jumping at you, his sword in front of him! He hits you straight in the chest! You stop abruptly as you find that William has defeated one guard! He was already charging at the one still remaining! You hear the sound of diamond clanging against diamond as the two swords hit each other! But unexpectedly, William kicks the guard, sending him flying down away from the entrance! He helps you up and tells you to get in the entrance while you still can! You find Al is following right behind you.

You open the door to find that you are on the outskirts of a jewel kingdom! Then you find that a few guards are on a wall surrounding the city! Before they can spot you, you run to the gate with the other soldiers and destroy the latch on the gate! You rush in to the beautiful city and spot something very interesting, a gym called "Lisa Doesn't Make You Lazy".

You shout, "Guys, look! This gem looks like the owner is the person we're looking for!" "Ok then, let's go!" says William.

You walk in to the gym to find a command block machine producing all of the training equipment. A lady with a collared shirt on and way too much makeup meets you.

Suddenly, she screams, "AHH! Griefer Empire Soldiers!!"

"*Oh snap, the only thing I forgot was a disguise*," you think to yourself.

You tackle the lady before she calls for security! But you find that you are too late! Lisa comes out, diamond sword drawn, with her Nyan Cat shirt on!

"You no good soldiers," she shouts as she hits you with her diamond sword! You tumble backwards as she helps up the lady with the collared shirt on.

William charges at Lisa, hitting her straight where her 6 pack is! She knocks Soldier 321 back with her powerful fists! But you get back up and attack Lisa on her unguarded side! She falls to the ground and then realizes that she is outnumbered and will be captured if she does not run away!

She and her customers all run outside to escape! Now that everyone is gone, you ask William and Al if they want to lift some weights. They both say they want to pump iron. So you decide to begin your first steps toward becoming John Cena.

William bench presses 200 pounds like it is a walk in the park. You decide to go with the fat man's version of the bench press, and rack up 85 pounds, and struggle to bench it with your spaghetti arms.

Al decides to go for a weight similar to his old name 877, and puts 87 pounds on the bar. He gets the bar half way up and can't hold it any longer. The bar comes down on his chest and squeezes it.

You and William scramble to help get the bar off of him. He sounds like a zombie and a yak at the same time as he yelps with a loud noise. You and William pick him up like the little baby he is, and carry him out of the gym only to meet a squad of guards ready to arrest you!

You watch as one of the soldiers grits his teeth. "Honey,

that's bad for your enamel," taunts William as he swings and connects his sword with the soldier!

Al, the crazy one, puts down some TNT, and commands you to run as he lights it! You watch as the number of soldiers depletes. You find one soldier crouching in the debris, badly injured. William goes over to finish him off, but you tell him to stop.

"Tell us where to find food, and we'll let you go," you bark at the lone remaining soldier. As quick as a flash, he hands you a business cards that reads, "The Diamond Deli: moded cakes, pork chops, steak, and all the fixin's"

Your heart jumps for joy and you tell William and Al, "Let's go!"

The three of you head toward the Diamond Deli. You open the door, sit down, and find that your server comes over immediately. You all take off your armor and put it in your inventories.

William is wearing a lava colored Adidas shirt to match his lava colored hair. Al is wearing a shirt that reads. "Bro, just chill" He also has a rainbow Mohawk. You look over the menu and narrow it down to either watermelon or mutton chops. Which do you choose?

TO ORDER WATERMELON, TURN TO PAGE 53

TO ORDER MUTTON CHOPS, TURN TO PAGE 52

GO AFTER COLLIN FIRST

Too bad Megan didn't give you a location for where these criminals are. You talk things over with the other two soldiers and decide to head west toward the setting sun. Sweat pours down your body as your armor turns into an oven and you climb slowly to the top of a mountain that you hope will give you a clear view of anything and everything nearby.

As you finally crest the top of the mountain, you spot two soldiers guarding a doorway built into the mountain.

You whisper, "Guys. Do you see those two guards down there?"

William shrugs his head, "Yes. I see them."

Al comes over and whispers, "How about we take them down. They don't look like friends."

You say quietly, "I've got a plan. You two go use your swords on the guards, and I'll stay up and snipe them with my bow and arrow!"

As soon as William hears the plan, he lunges down to the bottom of the mountain with his sword drawn, and takes a load of fall damage, but with all the force of the attack, he instantly destroys the first guard.

You shoot a flaming arrow right in the arm of the other soldier! He yowls in pain! Al sprints down the mountain! Unfortunately, he forgets to draw his sword, and the remaining soldier stabs him in his leg! But with all the health the remaining soldier had taken from your flaming arrow, Al is able to finish him off with just three punches!

Wounded and aching, Al has a look of relief on his face that his enemy has been defeated. William walks over and slowly pulls the sword out from Al's leg. Luckily, the armor was holding the injury in. As Al picks up the soldiers' drops weakly, he looks at a tag on one of the soldiers' helmets. It reads: "Collin's Jewel Army"

Al shouts excitedly, "These guys work for Collin, the guy we're looking for, right?"

"Evidently, yes," says William.

You ponder the evidence in your mind: a soldier wearing a "Collin's Jewel Army" helmet while guarding this cave entrance. This could get really exciting. The other two guys get very close to the entrance of the cave the soldiers were guarding and yell up to you: "Come on Steve!"

You walk cautiously down the mountain. "Stop being such a slow poke! It doesn't matter if you take half a heart of fall damage," says Al.

You jump and take no fall damage, and then walk into the doorway with Al and William.

Then you see what you could not have imagined in your wildest dreams: a village surrounded by glow stone, emeralds, gold, diamonds, and every other ore imaginable!! It's like a wonderland of jewels!!

But suddenly, you see what you were leaving out: a castle gatehouse made of diamond blocks with archers on top to protect the outer edge of the city.

The archers immediately realize you are not friends! They take out their bow and arrows and shower you with arrows from all directions! You and the rest of the soldiers dodge the arrows as your lives pass before your eyes and you pray you do not get caught. But there is a weakness in their attack: they are shooting too randomly. If you could dodge and then shoot your own arrows at the archers, then you could win this battle. You yell to the others, "Build a small shelter to cover us! Then build a stone hedge of protection at the top of it!"

The others begin frantically building the shelter as you take cover behind a rock and shoot arrows back at the enemy, picking off a couple of them! Once the shelter is built, you and the others climb up to where you can be protected and you whip out your bow and arrows and fire away! Every time you hit one of the soldiers, you imagine a little ringing sound to indicate you are getting more points! You clear the soldiers out and jump down into the inner layer of the mountain! You walk up to the gate of the gatehouse, but find that it is closed.

"Well, time to improvise," yells Al, as he pulls out a piece of flint and steel as well as a block of TNT. "Get back guys! This is, You run far and fast, and when it explodes, what seems like a sea of soldiers comes spilling out like ants on a log that's been turned over. Looks like you and your buddies are the exterminators!

"Retreat!" you cry. "No, I haven't done all that training for nothing," yells William as he draws his sword and starts taking out the enemy soldiers like he is clear cutting a forest! Seeing the warrior you have on your side, you decide to join him! Your sword comes out so fast, you are not even sure if you took it out yourself, and all in the same motion you begin to create a whirlwind of smoke and armor as you own the enemy soldiers and dismantle them piece by piece! Every time a soldier comes near you, he is brought to his knees!

And then when you finally get to the last soldier, William suddenly yells, "STOP!" He looks at the final soldier with mercy and says, "Tell us where we can get food, and we'll let you go!"

The enemy soldier drops to his knees and begs for mercy, and gives you a slip of paper, which looks like a business card and runs away in horror.

The card reads: "The Diamond Deli: moded cakes, pork chops, steak, and all the fixin's".

As soon as you all finish reading it, your swords crack in half! "Darn! I knew all that fighting would break my sword," shouts William as he walks over to the diamond gatehouse and starts dismantling it with his pick axe. "You and Al do the same," he continues.

After you're done with collecting the diamonds you need to

make another sword. You walk over to an unnatural tree with sparkling gold leaves, and mine the wood with your fists, take out a crafting table, and craft a brand spanking new sword. You walk on to the location imprinted on the business card that the enemy soldier gave you.

"We take a left at Miner's Haven, and we'll be there!" you exclaim.

A citizen runs swiftly past you! When he takes one look at your armor, he changes his speed from speed walking to sprinting!

"AAAAHHHH," he screams. "Griefer Empire Alert! Griefer Empire Alert!" He yells as he runs to tell other citizens. Al runs over to him, pulls out his sword and puts an end to him!

"Sorry, sir! But you were compromising the mission!" Al says coldly as he stands over the body and watches it turn into smoke and ash.

"OK! I for one, really need a drink of water after that," exclaims William. "I mean, do you really have to be that extreme, Al?"

As you and the rest of the guys walk toward The Diamond Deli, you think about how harsh this life is, and regret many parts of your past.

"I had to! Would you rather have Megan execute us for failing the mission?" yells Al.

"Well, all I'm saying is that you could have just threatened the guy without actually taking his life," replies William.

You jump in and say firmly, "You know what? You just need to end the conversation!"

"Agreed," William and Al say in unison.

As the conversation ends, you all arrive at The Diamond Deli, a site for sore eyes. It is made out of emerald and diamond ore! There are two blocks of emerald next to the door with two flower pots on them, one dandelion and one poppy. A sign above the door reads, "Service worth diamonds - No Griefers served"

"Better take off our armor, so they do not recognize us," you say.

The three of you take off your armor and put it in your inventories.

William is wearing a lava colored Adidas shirt to match his lava colored hair.

Al is wearing a shirt that reads, "Bro, just chill". He also has a rainbow Mohawk.

When you walk in to the deli, there are many different colored waiters running around. You notice that every waiter has an apron in the pattern of an ore. A hostess comes to greet you and gives you a piece of paper, which reads, "Color the diamond". She asks if you want crayons, but you know you don't have time to waste with those restaurant crayons from China that break as soon as you put pressure on the middle.

Al mutters under his breath to you, "Oh my goodness, she must be really tired to think you get a coloring sheet."

The hostess guides you to a table in the middle of the deli and says, "Your waiter will be right with you."

Five minutes later, your waiter finally arrives with some piping hot bread, and says, "Welcome to the Diamond Deli! My name is Shimmer, I'll be your server today."

You look over the menu and narrow your choices down, but you can't decide between mutton chops or watermelon. You know the waiter is coming back soon, so you'll have to make a choice.

TO ORDER WATERMELON, TURN TO PAGE 53

TO ORDER MUTTON CHOPS, TURN TO PAGE 52

MUTTON CHOPS

You decided to go with the mutton chops? Sorry. That's bad news. But there's also good news. The bad news is that you apparently do not recognize and hold in high regard the best food on God's green earth. But the good news is, we are going to let you live, and send you on the right path eating watermelon..

TURN TO PAGE 53, "WATERMELON"

WATERMELON

You tell the server, "Watermelon, please!" You think to yourself about whether or not that was a trick question. I mean, let me think here, a piece of meat or the best food in the entire world....a.k.a. God's gift to man. I mean, come on, right? Watermelon is the stuff! You know you have no choice as far as what you are drinking since the only drinks in Minecraft are potions that people rename with soft drink names. What a terrible world this is. I mean, where's the Gatorade or the Powerade? I'm working pretty hard here, people! What if your bars get extremely low and you're about to die?

Anyway....The waitress arrives with a complimentary appetizer you were not expecting: a trail mix. You grab a handful and pop some in your mouth quickly. You look at your inventory and above it, next to your character, you see "trail mix" with its picture next to it and for some reason you needed to pop your knuckles a bit, and as you do it, a fireball comes out of your hands! Woah! This is a wacky mod! What is this trail mix going to do next?

Then you think about the fact that there is a fire on the floor and it might burn up The Diamond Deli! But a waiter comes and extinguishes it with a dirt block.

You apologize to the waiter for making a fire and then take a little stroll. As you get outside the deli and begin your stroll, you realize you have crazy fast speed! *But there is one thing that stops you right in your tracks: wanted posters with your face and the faces of your friends on them!*

That guy that William let go, must have told about you! You try to put it out of your mind as you move down the sidewalk using your crazy fast speed.

An old woman walks by you and mutters, "Mods these

days," and shakes her head as she rolls her eyes and says, "When I first started my journey in this world, you were a pro if you found diamonds."

You see a miserable chicken roaming around the street, and run over to it in just a few quick steps, and punch it. With just one blow, you knock the chicken out of sight in a cloud of smoke and ash! WOW! You didn't know your own strength! You remember that you accidentally shot a fireball by cracking your knuckles, so you act like you're throwing something at the ground. Suddenly a fireball appears in your hand and you throw it! As soon as you throw it, you take a massive and unexpected jump! At your highest height, you see a beautiful palace with flags hanging all over it, which have the word "Collin" imprinted on them in blue. You have rocket jumping power too?! My goodness!! You leap back up again, and just for fun, shoot some fireballs at the flags and burn them to pieces!

Then as you land, you find that you have barely taken any fall damage because of one of the crazy powers of this mod, and you find a beautiful particle effect at your feet.

You decide that your food is probably waiting for you at the table, and you imagine it saying, "Come eat me, Steve. I am so juicy and ripe!"

"AHHH! Watermelon: the nectar of God," you think as you open the door to the deli.

When you get back to the table, you see your friends have already eaten!

"Dude! You were gone for like an hour!' shouts Al in disappointment.

You find your watermelon waiting for you as you planned, and chomp it down without a care in the world. Then you finally eat your way to the watermelon rind and let out a burp.

"I'm ready for the check.," you tell your friends.

"I'll go ask for it," says William. He comes back with a total Collin of 13 emeralds.

"I'll pay for it," Al says. "That guy I eliminated had 13

emeralds exactly. I'll pay for it with that."

You take the emeralds that Al gives you to the counter and pay.

"You look familiar," the waitress says in a thinking voice.

Remembering the "Wanted posters" with your face on them, you quickly reply innocently, "ME!? I'm just the average citizen."

Then the waitress starts in on you loudly and angrily, "I know you know what I'm talking about, and there are your friends over there too!!! You're with The Griefer Empire!!! I'm calling the guards in the chat now!!!"

You turn around cautiously and say in a sly tone, "That's not me.."

The waitress tries to alert the guards on chat, but when she is about to type it in, she says, "URGH! You can never get a wifi signal from here!"

She bolts to the back of the deli, which buys you enough time to craft a crafting table and craft a diamond axe on it.

Out of the corner of your eye, you see the waitress walking back into the front of the deli, still searching for a better wifi signal. But when she walks out of the door to what you think is the kitchen, you whirl around and throw your newly crafted axe right at her arm! "OWW!" she yells. "I'm only 13, you know?"

Like an expert, you pull out your bow and arrow and aim it at her. "Don't move a muscle, or I let go!" you shout. The only think you didn't suspect is that the waitress was tricking you the whole time about the wifi signal. You can see a message on your screen that reads, "From Hanna! Help me guards! I'm being attacked by a criminal!"

You drop to the floor in disbelief, your bow falls to the floor, and Hanna jumps over the counter, picks up your bow, and aims it at you. "Now who's laughing!" she says with revenge in her voice.

"Not you!" you yell at her as William and Al come to your

rescue. William grabs her and throws her against the wall, takes the bow from her hands, and gives it back to you.

"You don't mess with our friend!!" yells William.

Al helps you up and says to you, "Seriously bro?! That was a waitress. You could handle that."

"Well I can't handle her when she has a bow aimed at my head!" you reply.

Suddenly the guards bust open the front door and take out their bow and arrows and start firing! You block a few of the arrows with your sword.

To your surprise, they begin to yell, "Get away from Her Highness!"

"Huh!?" you reply bluntly.

One of the soldiers says, "You don't even know that she's the princess of Auria?"

"Nope, and I don't care either," you say as you begin firing flaming arrows at the soldiers.

Al and William go in for the attack! But there are just too many soldiers, and William and Al are overtaken! There are just too many soldiers. You keep firing away in desperation, one arrow after another gets you closer to your eventual inevitable capture. And sure enough, the soldiers close in on you as soon as you run out of arrows and they don't give you enough time to get out your sword and battle them .They take your inventory and tie your hands with lead. They take their swords out and tell you and your friends to move. They bring you to some horses they must have ridden in on and they throw you on.

A man who looks to be the leader of the guards asks you a question: "Do you know what this town is?" He pauses a moment and continues, "It's a town for rebels to hide and get weapons and other supplies. Megan sent you on the mission to eliminate its leader so the rebellion would almost fall apart. But now you have failed, and you will spend your time in a dungeon for the rest of your life."

"Don't be too sure of yourself! My friends and I may be smarter than you think, Captain Noob!" you snap back angrily.

The captain jeers back, "You get an extra week of rotten flesh for that one!"

When you arrive at the castle, you see the flags you scorched and smile. At least one thing went right today before it all went down the drain.

The castle has a moat, and like everything else in the town, the castle is made out of ores. As you come to the castle gate, a bored looking soldier says unenthusiastically, "State your reason for entry."

"Prisoner delivery, Ollie," says your captor. Ollie presses a button on a red stone mechanism and the gate opens.

You whisper your plan to your buddies: "William, you knock Ollie out with your sword, and set us free. Can you do that?"

"Yeah, I can do it," William whispers softly, and silently sneaks off of the horse. He walks over to Ollie and corndogs him! Ollie falls to the ground making an ouchie sound!

Like an expert, William steals Olliie's sword, and flings his sword through the air! It flies down and cuts through the lead, freeing his hands.

He takes Ollie's sword and challenges the captain, yelling, "Come on then! Are you a man or an amoeba, Captain Noob!"

Captain Noob appears to be up for the challenge and yells back, "Griefer scum! You think you could defeat me?"

William snaps back, "In easy, hard, and middle mode, Noob Muffin!"

Captain Noob looks so mad he could spit lava as he grabs his sword, stands up on his horse, and flies through the air with his sword in swinging position above his head, held by both his hands. As he comes down, he swings as hard as he can at William, who ducks and darts to the side, dodging his blow, and Captain Noob's sword gets stuck in the ground. He tries to pull it back out, to no avail as William whips out his sword and as he slays Captain Noob, yelling, "Whoopsies, you failed!"

But there is still one obstacle in William's way: the group of remaining soldiers. William wiggles his sword around in the soldier's face, and says, "Are you going to fight me, or are you too scared without your captain?"

One of the soldiers draws his sword, and lets out a battle cry, "Are any among us brave enough to fight this noob?"

"Hazzzaaaa!" they all yell, as they charge at William.

But William expertly summersaults over them and starts chopping them down one by one until they are all downed. He retrieves the items that they stole from your inventory and gives them back to you as he frees yours and Al's hands.

"Time for the boss fight! And there's no time to be stealthy since we've already been caught!" you yell.

You look at Al and know that when you call his name and give him the look, he'll know what to do.

"Al," you say in a you know what to do voice. Al walks over to the big gates to the castle, places the TNT right next to the gates to produce the most destruction on the inside, and lights it with flint and steel. BOOOOMM!!! The castle gates turn in to a giant gaping hole with tons of obsidian drop blocks! Al lets out a sinister laugh, which kind of creeps you out, and you walk in to what looks like the broken version of the main castle room. Tons of citizens with questions for Collin are running around in terror. There are only about four guards in the room and they are cowering in fear as well.

You see one guard trying to alert Collin in the chat. But you stop him and as you slay him you say, "Nope! Just nope!" On the left wall of the entrance, there is an item frame with a map of the castle in it. "If the employees only room is here, that's where we go," you say as you point at the map.

"Sounds like a plan to me! They might even have nova bombs and biome busters!" yells Al excitedly.

"There may be royal guardian swords and Mobzilla scale armor," says William as he rubs his hands together greedily.

"There might be king spawn eggs, queen spawn eggs, and Mobzilla spawn eggs to troll the enemy," you say with hope in your voice.

"Then let's stop talking about it and go there," says William impatiently. You run down the red stone floored hall! On your way, you pass a small prison hall. You look to see who has been imprisoned. It is all Griefer Empire Agents.

"Guys, come look at this!" you shout to your friends. Your friends drudge impatiently back to where you are.

"Oh wow! They're all Griefer Empire Guards?" says Al.

"Yes! And we need to break them out if we want some extra credit from Megan!" says William.

"With TNT?" Al says with a rise in his voice that lets you know he is more than ready to blow some more holes wherever he can.

"No! With our pick axes, you dummy!" you say as you shake your head.

But suddenly, two squads of soldiers come running at you with their swords drawn, looking more than a little bit upset!

"Al, you want to blow something up? Now's the time! Drop the TNT hammer! William, hold the other squad off as best you can!" you command.

You mine the obsidian jail as quickly as you can. But, even with a diamond pick ax, it still takes a long time to break. You hear the sounds of explosions and fighting going on, but you have no idea who is winning the battle!

Finally, you break through a small obsidian gap so the prisoner soldiers can be free and maybe even help you!!! Before you can say a word to the prisoner soldiers, they start to squeeze through the hole like they have grease on their bodies!!!! But after a few get through, you make the rest wait while you make the hole a little bigger.

The prisoner soldiers storm through the prison hall and take the enemy soldiers by storm!!!! You sit back and wish for a coke and popcorn as the prisoner soldiers exact revenge on

Collin's Minions!!! What a show!!!! Those who do not get taken out get thrown in their own slammer through the hole you created! Once they are all in, you cover the hole by building it back with obsidian blocks.

You rally up all of the soldiers by raising your sword high and yelling, "Let's defeat Collin and leave only smoke and dropped items!!!!"

The soldiers scream back their approval, "YOOOOOO!!!" as they raise their swords in the air with you.

You continue, "We need to give you guys some battle materials fit for the job!" You point with your sword and yell, "To the employees only room!"

The soldiers follow you down the hallway quickly and with great anticipation! You find the employees only room is blocked with a reinforced iron door. But this door is nothing compared to your gigantic mob!

"ATTACK!" you yell to the soldiers.

You stand back and watch the magic unfold!!! Your soldiers take their pick axes out and begin demolishing the door piece by piece until it caves in and falls apart. The first thing you see in the employees only room is a soldier crying because he knows he is at the mercy of your mob. You look at the soldier in a "Yes, it's about to happen" look, and drag him into the prison hall. You throw him in the prison, slamming the door behind him.

On the way back in to the employees only room, Will and Al have the eyes of kids in candy shops who just found the giant Haribo gummy bear. But instead of gummy bears, they have found tech guns! It isn't as good as the stuff you dreamed of, but you have never had the opportunity to try out the Tech Guns mod before! But it looks like Al's dream IS coming true. He has found a stack of nova bombs and biome busters! Al's eyes are as big around as saucers! What a sight! But it is not just Al who is in awe. You realize that you are going to get to choose your own weapon! Looking over your options, you see the bio gun, the nether blaster, and the golden revolver before you. The bio gun is lime green, filled with acid bullets, and the size of a mini gun. The nether blaster is a gray lava filled rifle. The golden revolver is a pistol size revolver that is James Bond's favorite weapon that shoots normal bullets.

The decision is tough, but the effects the bio gun has on enemies is unbelievable and something you want to experience! So you grab it as you watch Al and William pick their weapons of choice.

Al says, "Hey, William! Which one do you want?"

William looks him straight in the eye and says, "Is that a trick question?"

Al kind of looks him up and down and says, "I was giving you first choice, but if you want to ask questions, I'll make first choice!"

As he finishes his snippy sentence, Al reaches out and snares the nether blaster and says, "It'll go perfect with my bombs and explosive mindset!"

"Then I guess I'll go with the Golden Revolver, James Bond style," says William as he shoots it at the ceiling just to get a couple laughs.

Eager to get things moving along, you say, "So now let's not leave these poor hostages hanging." You dig deeper in the weapons chest to find a stack of laser rifles to give to the hostages. "Before we make a full scale attack, let's find our way around this castle," you declare.

Suddenly, a small squad of soldiers with one big soldier leading them, walk angrily toward you.

"It's time to test these weapons!" you yell to the group. William aims and fires at one snarling soldier right next to the big one! He falls to the ground instantly! Then William finishes him off with two quick shots.

"*It's your turn now,*" you think to yourself, as you aim your gun at the biggest soldier. You take a shot right around his belly button and watch the acid sizzle.

The rest of the mob has their own little fight with the average sized soldier while you and your buddies finish off the biggest one.

The big guy makes a long range punch, not intending to hit any of you specifically. Al expertly cartwheels over the soldier's fist and fires a flaming bullet at his shoulder. Now the soldier is all William's as he finishes him off with one quick shot! He falls to the ground in a dramatic way as smoke and ashes come off his body. You look over and see that your army has easily vaporized the enemy soldiers.

"Too bad there isn't a way we could get rid of this room extremely quickly," Al says sarcastically as he pulls a Nova Bomb slowly from his inventory, puts it down, lights it with flint and steel, and runs. He watches the Nova bomb suck in the blocks and spit them back out.

"Where'd it go, I could've thought it was there before?" he says sarcastically again.

Suddenly you see a hooded figure dash by and drop an enchanted book on the floor. "Who was that?" you quickly ask.

"Who? I didn't see anybody," says William.

You say, "Look, look! He's right there!"

"I think you're seeing things, Steve," Al says.

You reply sharply, "NO! I'm not!"

William kneels down and looks at the enchanted book. "What's this?" he asks. "Yes, yes! He dropped that when he ran by!"

William opens the book and finds that it reads: "Hello, my name is Collin. I know your names: William, Steve, and Al. If you want to find me, you will have to look where pumping is loud. If you need a hint, you will have to win it at this place." The next page is torn off, leaving you wondering what was on it. Al has been puzzling the whole time you are reading.

"Perhaps it means the place where they pump air into bicycle tires?" says Al.

"Of course not, genius! What kind of answer is that? There

are barely any bicycles in Minecraft!" William says. "It obviously means....uh....uh...uh....I'm not very good at riddles."

You puzzle and think for what feels like hours, and finally come up with a reasonable answer: "The plumber's house!"

"Great job, Steve!" says William. "Let's just forget about this, and just blow the place to bits, and not care if we destroy Collin." says Al.

"Fine! That's just fine! Let's just go on and think of a more reasonable plan," you say. You order your mob to follow behind you as you get ready to cause some destruction. But as you take out your bio gun, you finally find the obvious thing you need.

"We need help, guys," you say.

"Well that's great! Do you know who has the page? No, you don't!" says Al.

"Hold on, one sec! The first soldier we find, we will force information out of!"

You see an important looking Commander with a shotgun out of the corner of your eye. "You see that guy, William? He's yours," you tell William.

William punches his hand and says sternly, "He'll end up like Captain Noob when I'm done with him." He runs at the commander and as he notices William and fires his shotgun, William spins around skillfully with an axe in hand, and when he comes out of his spin, he throws the axe! The axe hits the commander's shotgun and breaks it!

He takes out his own tech gun and aims it at the commander, yelling, "Stand down!"

The commander whimpers like a puppy with his hands up.

"Tell us where your noob king hid the page that was ripped out of this enchanted book," William yells as he throws the book down angrily.

He reluctantly and fearfully mumbles, "The Fourth Ballista Spa. It's in the castle. I warn you: it's the king's private spa and top class soldiers guard it at all times."

"Oh, like you?" says William, looking at him and poking

fun.

"I'm so scared," William jokes and shakes his hands to be dramatic.

"Do not underestimate me, griefer weakling," the Commander snaps back.

"Careful! I can pull the trigger on this at any time!" says William to the Commander. "Anyways, thanks for your help, whatever your name is! Now I'm afraid I'm going to have to put you in an obsidian cage with a TNT trap on it for anyone dumb enough to come rescue you," William says.

"You wouldn't," the Commander says.

"Oh, yes I would!" says William as he starts to build the cage.

"I'm the closest there is to being the King's Royal Guard," the Commander says.

"Well, not anymore! You'll most likely rot away in this cage," replies William.

Continuing to make fun of the Commander, William looks around at you and Al and says, "All right everyone, rank up because Commander Noob has failed."

The Commander fires back: "If you are a leader, then you are a failure on every level of leadership."

William gets the last word as he shoves him into the obsidian cage and says, "Bye, bye! I hope you enjoyed your last conversation!"

William walks back with a smirk on his face and says, "What did I tell you? Now let's go find the Fourth Ballista Spa!"

You and your friend run out of the castle with your army at your side! But, to your surprise, as you open the golden doors of the castle's exit, a bullet flies right by you! You immediately whip out your nether blaster and look for the gunman-and then you find him-or should I say them? You watch as soldiers pop in and out of cover while firing, like a whack-a-mole game gone scary.

Suddenly, you feel a deep anger well up in your blood, and

it seems to empower you to shoot your nether blaster right into one of the soldiers! He falls down in a whirlwind of ash and smoke and disappears!

William seems to have the same anger welling up inside of him as well. He whips out his golden revolver, like the Minecraft version of Marshall Dylan, and manages to hit a few soldiers while missing the rest.

"I feel like I know the tool for this job," Al says. "And, of course, everyone knows what it is: some good ole Nova Bombs!!!"

Al ignites one nova bomb, kicks it in the air, and it lands right where the soldiers are! The nova bomb sucks the soldiers in and takes them out!

"Okay, let's go before more come!" you shout.

"Oh, come on! Nobody's going to pat me on the back or anything?" yells Al.

Suddenly, a shotgun comes flying at you! You grab it with one hand, and examine it. "Must have been one of the soldier's," you think to yourself. I guess it won't take too much inventory space with one gun. So you take the gun, and you, your friends, and your army head out for the stables in order to get some transportation to go to the Fourth Ballista Spa.

You all saddle up your horses and take off! Thank goodness! You are finally on your way to the spa! As you ride along, you think about how long it has been since the last time you ate. Your energy bars are really low, but you soldier on. Finally, off to your left, you see a giant wheat field with a path made of cobblestone running through it, which leads up to The Fourth Ballista Spa. You begin to ride up the cobblestone pathway, feeling the relief that you are finally arriving when your horse nays. In a matter of moments, every horse begins to nay.

"What's wrong, girl?" you ask your horse. But then, you see it: green lumbering bodies creeping through the wheat field! Oh my goodness! *This could get ugly,* you think to yourself. You take out your newly found shotgun and blast the zombie back to where he came from! Your soldiers take out their guns and begin to fire away as well, but some are taken down by the return fire.

"Snipers! They're in the trees!" Al yells.

You take out your bio gun and fire straight at the leafy parts of the trees.

"William!" you shout, "I'm going to need you to take out those snipers while we handle the zombies! Take a small group of soldiers with you!"

"Yes, sir!" William says as he salutes you. "Come on men!" he shouts to the soldiers. He continues, "Anyone want to join me?"

Immediately a squad lines up single file behind William.

"Cover me!" William shouts as he storms through a flurry of zombies!

The soldiers easily put the zombies out of their misery; but, you never underestimate the zombies because their strength is in their numbers. Suddenly, a zombie comes only a few inches away from William! Surprised, William takes out his revolver and drops the zombie!

"Come on men, Come on! Faster!" William yells.

Suddenly a sniper shoots right at William, who dodges it like an expert. But it hit one of his soldiers and wounded him critically.

"You'll pay for that, you no good rebel!" yells the downed soldier. The soldier takes out his rifle and blasts the enemy sniper! The sniper disappears in a cloud of ash and smoke!

"One sniper down, two to go!" William shouts triumphantly. "I'll take this one!" he shouts confidently. He runs through the wheat field, slicing and dicing zombies along the way! Finally, he reaches the tree where the sniper dwells! He climbs up the tree like Tarzan, and before the sniper knows what happened, he is kicked off the tree and incurs too much fall damage to continue! The other sniper is not focused on

William, so William has no trouble in taking out his golden revolver and destroying the sniper!

"Mission accomplished, Steve!" William says. "Now let's make our way toward the Fourth Ballista Spa."

You examine the building, and find there seem to be no defenses or booby traps of any kind; however, the entry door is barricaded with two iron doors. Yep, they were definitely preparing for you, you think to yourself.

"Al, you know what to do," you say as you wave him forward. Al takes out a nova bomb, and does what he does best: BOOM!!! The door blows wide open, along with a ton of other debris!

You run inside the building and find people dancing; yet, at the same time there are soldiers with guns guarding the whole area. Out of the whole place, you recognize 3 people: Collin, Ben, and Lisa. They are targets given to you by Megan and The Griefer Empire. You immediately organize a plan for your army to take out the guards while you, William, and Al take Collin, Ben, and Lisa hostage. The fight is on!!

William goes straight for Lisa, Al goes for Ben, and you go for Collin! Ben and Al charge at each other head first! Collin takes out a rifle and starts firing at you! Lisa and William run at each other, and skillfully do a number of karate moves on each other!

"Come on, and fight like a man!" Collin orders you. "Okay, you want me to fight like a man? Here you go!" You jump in the air, and kick the rifle right out of Collin's hands!

"You, little....," Collin says angrily.

"What are you going to call me, a noob? I disagree!" you yell as you fire your shotgun at Collin.

"Hey! It took me a while to craft that shotgun, you know!" Collin yells at you, as he lunges to steal the shotgun.

"Well, it's mine now!" you yell as you knock him to the ground with your shotgun. You take your shotgun and aim it right at him! "Surrender or die! It's over now! Your army's going to fall along with all your rebellious friends!"

Collin shouts, "I'll never give in to the Griefer Empire! Join me and you'll be better off! I can sense the power of your need to be free inside you!"

You feel a force pulling inside you and say, "Maybe you're right, but I'm not going to join the rebels just yet."

Ben and Al are still going at each other, swords clanking. Al suddenly whirls around and jabs his sword with extra power, sending Ben flying back in agony. Ben gets back up, angry as a hornet! He runs back and body slams Al! Ben takes out a crossbow, and fires at Al's legs! But, just in time, Al gets back up, and blocks it with his diamond sword! Al charges at Ben, sword first, and slices at Ben's hands furiously! Ben grabs the sword, but Al still does not waste this attack. As Ben holds on to the sword, Al grabs the handle and hurls Ben behind himself!

Ben, with his breath knocked out of him, speaks softly and desperately with a strong country accent, "Al, I know we've had a battle, but we can still be friends."

"Never! I've been in the glorious military for 11 years now!" yells Al.

"Although I do see what you're meaning, I would like some freedom once in a while. Think about it," Ben mumbles as he falls into a daze.

Al paces back and forth thinking about his options. Meanwhile, Lisa and William are fighting tooth and nail against each other! William crane kicks Lisa! But, she grabs his foot, and sends him spinning backwards!

In midair, she pulls out her laser pistol, and blasts William! But William doesn't even touch the ground. He puts his hands down as he falls, and pushes himself back up. A look of fury comes over him as he approaches Lisa, his golden revolver in hand. He shoots Lisa! As she endures the pain, William punches her, knocking her backwards in defeat. She crawls over to William, and in one of those, "I'm a crossfit trainer voices", she says, "You'd be a great addition to the Rebellion!"

"Why?" William questions with a sense of pride in his voice.

"Because, you're so powerful! I couldn't even beat you!" And with that, she passes out on the floor. The soldiers are about to finish off the rest of the guards, but you decide you need to make a decision as you see Collin coming to.

You tell Collin, "Tell your guards to stop fighting, and I will do the same with my soldiers! We may decide to join the Rebellion!"

Collin makes it to his feet, and both of you yell, "STOP! STOP! Soldiers stop the fighting!"

As the fighting stops, and the soldiers look at the two of you in disbelief, you tell William and Al to come talk with you. Both William and Al look weary from battle, but they come to your side, and you say, "It's time for us to make our decision, guys. This could change our friendships around or it could make a great alliance. It is time for us to make a choice between the Griefer Empire and The Rebellion. We have been fighting for the Griefer Empire forever now. Maybe it's time to make a change and get our freedom back."

William looks at you and says, "I agree."

Al chimes in and nods, saying, "We don't have long to decide. What do you think, Steve?"

TO STAY WITH THE GRIEFER EMPIRE, TURN TO PAGE 70

TO JOIN THE REBELLION, TURN TO PAGE 71

THE GRIEFER EMPIRE

Collin approaches you from behind and asks hopefully, “So, have you decided to join us?”

“Uh, nope! All that stuff we said was just a plain lie, and you were too dumb to not see it. This world needs structure and order! Why would we ever join you?”

Suddenly, Lisa wakes up from her forced nap, and she must have had a dream about attacking William because she pins William to the wall and puts to an end to him right in front of your eyes!! OH NO!

Ben is out of his daze now, and comes charging at Al! Ben’s surprise attack takes Al by storm, and he throws Ben far beyond The Fourth Ballista Spa!!

You find that the enemy soldiers have dishonored orders, and start picking off your soldiers one at a time with shotguns, rifles, swords, and whatever weapons they can find in their inventories.

How quickly your army has been reduced to ONE, only YOU.

“You’re a traitor!” Collin shouts at you as he kicks you to the ground and destroys you with his diamond sword!

THE END

THE REBELLION

"So, what have you decided?" Collin asks you.

"We've decided to join The Rebellion!" you tell him with a sense of relief.

"Good choice! We don't have much time! My spies tell me that Megan is coming to you because of how long you have been gone. With your power and support of this rebellion, we might just keep this city alive."

WOW! Megan is powerful enough to destroy a city full of armed rebels, you think to yourself.

"So, what's your plan?" you ask Collin.

He lays out a piece of paper, a feather, and ink. "Okay. Here's our city," says Collin as he draws a quick doodle of what is supposed to be a city. "We're here, and Megan is here," says Collin as he points and draws an evil face to represent Megan. "My plan is to make a gigantic barricade with our soldiers and the rebels in town. Ben, you'll command those troops."

Ben looks happy, and says, "Yeah, we'll turn her big chunky body guards into mashed potatoes!"

"The rest of us will be at a mountain, here," Collin says as he points to the map. "While Ben and his troops are distracting Megan, we'll take her out!"

"Sounds like a risky plan to me! That's the kind I like!" Al says in excitement.

"But, before we put this plan into action, we need to get you guys fed," says Collin as he open a door to a huge banquet filled with butlers and maids at the ready.

You hadn't seen a meal like this in days. You take a seat at the table along with everyone else, and right after you pray, you immediately start yelling, "Pass the mutton chops, please! Pass the mutton chops, please!"

"Sure," Ben says as he takes a baked potato and passes you the mutton chops.

You grab a mutton chop like it was running away from you! William takes his time and indulges in the watermelon and mushroom stew. Collin nibbles on a golden carrot, and with every bite he seems to grow more alive.

"I am stuffed," you say. Your hunger bars are completely replenished, and you still want dessert. One of the butlers brings out a beautiful golden apple cake topped with a cookie for everyone. You take your cookie and your slice and savor the strength giving cake. You look down at your hearts and find that you have two extra golden hearts. "That's what anything golden apple will do to you," you say.

"Is everyone good and ready for the battle?" Collin asks.

"Ready as ever!" Lisa says as she pumps her fists.

"Then let's head to the battlefield," Collin shouts as a maid opens the door and everyone heads out.

You look out in a battlefield, and you see two men riding on a horse: one old and wise, and one young and athletic. When they come closer, you realize who they are: famous warriors who defeated countless evil beings of the nether. Now they are going to help you and your friends? The two men jumped off the horses as quickly as possible.

"I came here as quickly as I could, Collin," the young man says in an Australian-American accent.

"We need to rally up all the rebels in the city," Collin says. "Steve, you go with him, and meet up in the town square. Then we will execute our plan."

You and the young man rush off for the houses in the village. Suddenly, you realize that the sun is setting, and you and the young man must round up the rebels before dark or you might have a fight on your hands!

You see one house, which you know is a rebel's house, because it has two item frames above the door that have the syllables of the word rebel.

"Well, they aren't afraid of the Griefer Empire, now are they?" you say. You open the door and find they are ready: a teenager with war paint on and wielding a diamond sword greets you at the door.

"Oh, is it time for battle? I'll go tell my parents," says the teenager with conviction. He calls his parents, and you find the mother armed with a flamethrower and wearing a pink dress.

"Honey! It's time to slay the Griefer Empire!" she yells. A lumbering man walks out with an old fashioned hunting rifle.

"One family down...probably tons more to go," you say. The young man shows no emotion toward you.

"We have work to do, Steve. Let's go!" says the young man.

Suddenly, you hear a groaning noise. You know that sound from a mile away: ZOMBIES!!!

A zombie lumbers toward the teenager! But the teenager expertly slices it in half with his diamond sword! Three more zombies head toward his parents! The father takes down one of the zombies with his hunting rifle! The mother unleashes the flamethrower on the rest of the zombies, turning them into a puddle that looks like melted ice cream!

You see yet another house with item frames above the door that read, "You want a homemade knuckle sandwich, Griefer Empire?"

You open their door and find that it is only a man and a woman, but they look like great warriors! The man has two shotguns on his back, a patch on his eye, and two diamond swords in sheaths. The woman looks like a friend of Al's, with two grenades and some on her belt.

Then you see the biggest house in the village other than the castle! It looks to be a mansion, probably filled with people for your army! You walk up to it and find that these people also have a strong hatred for the Griefer Empire.

On the entrance to the mansion, there are item frames displaying Griefer Empire helmets that have been spray painted or shot at. You open the door and are greeted by someone with the best gear you have ever seen.

There is a man wearing Royal Guardian Armor and wielding an enchanted Ultimate Sword standing there looking at you. Behind him, you see a family of 20, all dressed and armored like him.

“We’re ready!” says the man who greeted you in an aggressive tone of voice.

Suddenly, something you could have never imagined is happening right in front of you: MOBZILLA is spawned right in front of you!!!!!

Within seconds, it smashes the mansion to pieces!!! You are glad these guys have Royal Guardian armor on because this is going to be a BIG fight!!!!

You take out your bio-gun even though you know it will be practically useless! You fire it anyway! But, as you suspected, the bio-gun is doing very little to help your cause!

The young man comes in and tries to attack MOBZILLA but is thrown back by its fireball attack!! The family wearing Royal Guardian Armor comes in slicing at MOBZILLA’S feet, inflicting damage!!

Suddenly you find that rebels from other houses have come to join you in your fight!!!!! You see one sporting the ultimate bow, others using normal bows, and one looks to be sending down a missile!!!!!

“DAAANNNNNGG!!!” you think to yourself!. *This town is very modded!”*

You watch as MOBZILLA’S health depletes rapidly. But then you hear it: the sound of Royal Guardian armor breaking!! The family’s armor is destroyed!! The person with the ultimate bow fires at MOBZILLA, but MOBZILLA deflects the arrows with his tail!!!!

Finally, the missile one of the rebels fires hits the ground, and MOBZILLA cries out like a dinosaur who just got bit!!!! MOBZILLA finally falls to the ground, defeated!!!

Every victor raises their weapons high in the air, shouting

like they just took down Jericho!!!!

But then your counterpart stops the excitement and tells you to stand at attention to be counted.

"Ok, so we have around 90 soldiers," says the young man. "Long range soldiers, you will be up top with Collin and the rest. Melee troops, you'll be with myself, Steve, and Ben," the young man orders. "Now let's go back to the battlefield! Any of you who are not armored, go to the armory to armor up!"

You see the family of 20, and a few others disband from the group and head to the armory. They come back in a few minutes, some dressed in emerald, others dressed in diamond. You head to the front lines where Ben stands wearing his emerald armor, his emerald sword drawn. You see a few butlers from the feast in the distance, some armed with bows and diamond armor, others with armor and swords. Everyone is ready for the battle against The Griefer Empire to go down!

Suddenly, Collin orders you to come to his position, high atop a hill, on a plateau looking down on a pathway to the city. It is a perfect place for long range sniper fire. You make your way to the position with Collin and Al, who has a nether blaster, TNT, flint, and steel at the ready. You see a few other soldiers crouching behind an obsidian wall that guards them from Griefer Empire fire. You see the man with his hunting rifle, the person with the ultimate bow, and a few butlers.

And then you see it: what looks like the Axis Powers, and you are the Allied Forces. Leading from the front of the Griefer Empire is Megan, dressed in obsidian battle armor with four big, chunky bodyguards guarding her.

In the slightest voice Collin says to his troops, "FIRE!!" Within seconds, arrows, bullets, biogun bullets, and fireballs, and grenades fly through the air inflicting damage on the Griefer Empire!!!!!

You see a few Griefer Empire soldiers drop!!! But then you realize that some of the soldiers have Ultimate Swords! You must defeat them quickly while you have the element of surprise!

You pick one off, and he falls to the ground. But then Megan notices you! She sends out five big chunky guys toward your group! But William stands in front of them, blocks their way, and takes them down with his golden revolver!

Ben and the rest of his squadron charge at the Griefer Empire, every weapon they own being put to good use!!

A few Griefer Empire soldiers appear to be archers as they take down a few rebels! Ben takes a dastardly shot to the shoulder! But before one of the archers can finish him off, William shoots one of them!

You keep firing at one of Megan's bodyguards, and finally he disappears!

Suddenly, you see the man with the eye patch and two diamond swords defeat two of Megan's bodyguards, but Megan immediately fights back against the man with the eye patch and defeats him!!! She takes out her bow, and with her expert archery skills drops 3 rebel soldiers like they were bad habits!! 3 other rebel soldiers try to counterattack, but are defeated by Griefer Empire soldiers using their Ultimate Swords!

Luckily, they haven't seen you yet, and you manage to pick off the whole row of Griefer Empire soldiers!! But you know you are still overpowered by the Griefer Empire.

Megan keeps destroying one rebel soldier after another until she finally gets to William. "Traitor, you'll die for your treason against the Griefer Empire!" Megan shouts at William.

"What was that? I couldn't hear. Did you say the noob empire?" William taunts back.

With that, Megan lashes out with her obsidian sword, striking William down!! But before he hits the ground, he manages to get one shot off to hit her with his golden revolver!! She soldiers on despite being badly hurt, and raises her obsidian sword to finish off William.

But before she can do it, you jump out of your sniper spot, sword drawn, yelling, "For the Rebellion!" You can't hear all of the voices saying, "Don't do it, Steve!! Don't jump down there!!"

You jump in front of Megan, taking a large amount of fall damage and placing yourself in harm's way, and quickly slam your sword against Megan's obsidian battle armor and hear a loud CLANG! With all the power behind that hit, Megan's obsidian chest plate is almost broken!

She counters with a near death blow straight to your helmet, which clatters to the ground, broken!

But you are in full beast mode now! You pull yourself up and feel like fire is in your eyes! You attack as fast as a lightning bolt hitting a creeper! With the first hit, Megan's chest plate breaks! With the second hit, her health is lowered significantly!! With the third hit, she is at half a heart!!! You kick her into a patch of lava created by one of her own soldiers!!!! But she jumps out as fast as lightning before you can finish her off, and runs away like an ocelot running from a Minecrafter who needs a cat!! You have won the battle for now!!!

You fall to the ground exhausted, and hear the celebratory cries of victory as everyone runs toward you, giving you big hugs, and raising you up!!!

You wake up from your slight nap and watch as Collin gives you a thumbs up, and then watch as the rest of the rebels destroy or capture the remaining enemy soldiers!!!

The cries of victory can be heard all around you! Today is your day of victory!!

Once the cries of victory fade away, Collin comes over and says, "Steve, Al, and William, I want you in my office for another mission. As you know, Megan and other Griefer Empire leaders are still out there and we have to destroy them and overthrow their rule." You think about how you are now a hero of the rebels, and how one day the evil Griefer Empire will fall forever!!!!

TO BE CONTINUED IN BOOK TWO......

CHEST THREE

You open chest number 3 with your fingers crossed, hoping to find something awesome! Your optimism turns into joy as you crack the chest open to reveal a diamond sword worthy of being used by the best soldiers in the land! This weapon will surely be at your side from now on! Along with the sword you find DIRT! Thank goodness! The dirt is just what you need to get back out of the ditch!

You decide to build a staircase and confront the soldiers now that you have a sword! As you build the staircase, you think about how the fight is going to go down: first you will spot them, and the element of surprise will be in your favor because they will not see you coming at them; but, you know that battles never go the way you predict. You just hope you will win! And the element of surprise is what you need to have the upper hand.

As you build the last step of the stair case, you crouch down and peek above ground to see if you see the soldiers. There they are! You catch a quick glance of them before popping your head back down. They are walking around and all you could hear them say before you pull your head back was, "pork chops".

So, you plan it out quickly in your mind, and go for it! You launch yourself at one of the troopers, swing your sword, and send him flying into a cactus outside!

"That was the end of him," you say.

"You'll pay for that!" says the other trooper as he angrily thrusts his sword into yours! You both battle it out with your sword skillfully until you get a break through! You slam your sword so hard against the trooper's sword that his sword flings through the air! While his sword is still in the air, you roll behind him, grab his head, and slam it full force into your knee. He falls on to the ground, KO'd.

"That's right! Yeah boyyy," you yell! Now that you have worked the two troopers over, it is time to go down and find out what is in chest #4. So, you run back down the steps you built and get back to the chests.

You open up chest #4, feeling one part hopeful and one part fearful, kind of like the first day of school when you are a little kid. As the chest cracks open, the first thing you see is a shimmering silver reflection! It's a sword fit for someone who slays evil just like yourself! You also find a ladder, a bow, and a stack of arrows. SCORE!! You make your way back up the staircase, full of pride and a sense of relief.

Time to build your shelter! You decide to build a house. You are not sure if you should build a cobblestone house or a log cabin. You sit down to think about it....

TO BUILD A COBBLESTONE HOUSE, TURN TO PAGE 103

TO BUILD A LOG CABIN, TURN TO PAGE 104

CHEST FOUR

You open up chest #4, feeling one part hopeful and one part fearful, kind of like the first day of school when you are a little kid. As the chest cracks open, the first thing you see is a shimmering silver reflection! It's a sword fit for an evil slayer like yourself! You also find a ladder, a bow, and a stack of arrows. You gladly add them to your inventory and build a staircase out of the ditch!

As you build the last step of the stair case, you crouch down and peek above ground to see if you see the soldiers. There they are! You catch a quick glance of them before popping your head back down.

They are walking around and all you could hear them say before you pulled your head back was, "Pork chops".

You realize the only way to move forward is to eliminate these guys. So, you plan it out quickly in your mind, and go for it!

You launch yourself at one of the troopers, swing your sword, and send him flying into a cactus outside!

"That was the end of him!" you yell.

"You'll pay for that!" shouts the other trooper as he angrily thrusts his sword into yours!

You both battle it out with your sword skillfully until you get a break through! You slam your sword so hard against the trooper's sword that his sword flings through the air. While his sword is still in the air, you roll behind him, grab his head, and slam it full force into your knee. He falls on to the ground KO'd.

"That's right! Yeah boyyy," you yell.

Time to build your shelter! You decide to build a house. You are not sure if you should build a cobblestone house or a log cabin. You sit down to think about it....

TO BUILD A COBBLESTONE HOUSE, TURN TO PAGE 103
TO BUILD A LOG CABIN, TURN TO PAGE 104

LEFT PATH

You choose the path to the left because you think it will be the best path. Fear grips you as you sprint at top speed toward safety!

When you finally run out of breath, you slow down to a panting walk as you slowly look around to keep yourself safe. You start to think about how your life could end tonight, and you think about how sad it would be to pass away on a hillside that you have never been on before. It is just sad that your life has come to this point. But at the same time, you know that there is hope, and you are clinging to that hope with all you have as you walk up the hill toward what you hope is the mayor's house.

Suddenly, a spider comes at you! You dodge a blow from the spider as he misses you and gets knocked out for a few moments, which gives you time to see a band of chunky men with swords all around their belts.

They come over chanting, "I got you where I want ya! Now, I'm gonna eat ya!"

You turn around and see the zombies have caught up with you and you quickly try to change the subject and yell, "Maybe you could eat these mobs! I'm not tasty at all!"

They all shout, "Okay!" You are thankful these guys are not very intelligent. They each take a sword out of their belt, stab the mobs, and use them as kabobs. But, they eat the rotten flesh and die. *Could this scenario have ended any better*, you think? Absolutely not!

Now you know you took the best path, or did you take the wrong path and use your smarts to make it the best path? Either way, you find yourself grabbing two swords from each of the three chunky men for a total of six swords, and you scarf down potatoes and carrots from the remains of the zombies. Like a savage, you have survived unharmed. With your health restored from the food and your safety increased by having the swords, your spirits pick up as you head farther up the path.

Looking around you as you hike farther up the hill, you notice an oddly shaped shack. You think to yourself, *this might be the home of the three chunky guys who met their demise.*

Walking toward the shack with great caution, you see a fat juicy cow and pig. Looks like somebody lives here.

You walk up very slowly to the shack door, and begin to nudge it open slowly....creeeeaaaaakkkk. The door to the shack creaks open and you walk in to find two chests and a mine cart that leads to someplace unknown. Hmmmm. You think about your choices for a few moments. What do you want to do?

TO OPEN THE CHEST CLOSEST TO YOU, TURN TO PAGE 83

TO OPEN THE CHEST FARTHEST FROM YOU, TURN TO PAGE 88

TO GET ON THE MINECART, AND SEE WHERE IT LEADS, TURN TO PAGE 90

THE CLOSEST CHEST

You open the chest and see an enchanted axe called "The Meal Maker". You think, *"What am I supposed to do with this?"*

But your thoughts stop abruptly when you hear a loud explosion!! You fall into a hard cobblestone floor! You hear chanting and screaming and the sound of popcorn popping.

You look up to see a whole arena full of big chunky guys that look like the ones you met on the path up the hill. You look across where you came from to see a group of the chunky men behind a gate and realize you are in a gladiator arena!!!

Feeling like you may have to defend yourself, you take one of the swords from your inventory and hold it tight, ready to fight! A man who looks like a ref opens the gate and the big chunky guys charge at you!

You spin and stab the first big chunky guy as hard as you can! He falls to the ground with a thud and with smoke and ashes coming out of his body, he disappears! You think to yourself, *did I really just do that?* The crowd cheers for you!

The ref yells, "Full charge!!" The remaining group of chunky men come running at you head first and you slide under their wide open legs, a move known in soccer as a nutmeg! You thought they would keep charging and run into the arena, but they stopped just before hitting their heads on the arena wall. You quickly throw the sword at the leader of the pack, hitting him straight in the head! He falls down and turns into a heap of smoke and ashes, a sight you welcome with eager anticipation!

You run to grab your sword to finish off the remaining four big chunky guys! You slam your sword into one of the big chunky dudes, slamming him into his partner like a rolling bowling ball! They both disappear with ashes and smoke coming out of them! You thought this tactic would work for the other two, so again you try to plunge your sword into the first of the two guys, but he grabs it and punches you in the face, sending you half way across the arena! The crowd cheers loudly for the big chunky guy as he bows his back and raises his hand in the air like he will be victorious! You think to yourself, *"I have to win this battle."*

You take another sword from your inventory and charge at the big chunky guy! He sends a flying punch at you, but you dodge it with ease. This missed punch slows him down and makes him vulnerable. You use this opportunity to plunge your sword into him, sending him all the way into the arena stands! One of the fans catches him and winds up with a pile of ash and smoke on him.

With only one chunky enemy left, you run at him and jump, and send a flying kick to his face, which sends him flying to a sewage drain in the middle of the arena floor. His weight opens the grate on top of the drain and he falls into the sewage drain hole, flying downward!

The crowd gasps and a loud "OOOOOOHHHHHHH!" is heard as smoke and ash raises up through the drain hole!

Suddenly, you spot a skinny man in the crowd with a dark hood on, sitting in a fancy red chair fit for a king. You realize he IS the king. And he looks you right in the eye with anger, raises his arm, and makes a motion with his hand across his neck like he is cutting it with a knife, stands up, makes the cut throat motion again and yells to the crowd in a dark, evil, and loud voice, "ATTACK!!"

All of the big chunky guys in the crowd jump down into the arena and charge at you! But, in the blink of an eye, the gate breaks down and 113 soldiers come stomping in with swords drawn, and you know this is going to be a nasty scene! As the soldiers enter the arena for battle, they realize they need to change weapons, and quickly. With precision speed, they whip out their bow and arrows, and the king yells to the big chunky guys, "Switch weapons to bow and arrows!" The big chunky guys fire at the soldiers! The soldiers dodge the arrows with great precision and they shoot their own bows and arrows, and make a direct hit on all of the big chunky guys!

The king looks on in shock, and yells, "NO!"

One of the soldier leaders throws you a bow and arrow dabbed in weakness potion. He yells at you with a British accent, "Aim for the king!!!"

You aim as best you can at the king's chest, fire, and your arrow catches the king in the shoulder! He is weakened because of the potion on the arrow, which gives time for the soldiers to finish off the king. But as they fire arrows at the king, he makes a dark shield out of his hands and blocks the arrows.

The king runs away as fast as he can, escaping the arena with only a wound to the shoulder. Although his escape was not the ending you wanted, you and the soldiers consider it a victory and raise your arms in the air in triumph, yelling, "AHHHHHHHH!!!! WE ARE VICTORIOUS!!"

But there is still a part of you that feels unsettled as you ask the soldier next to you, "Where do you think the king went?"

In a British accent, the soldier replies, "Should we go after him or just get out of here?"

You find yourself torn as to what to do. These guys who saved you may also lead you to your death if you go after the king. But if you try to get away, you are a bigger target when traveling in a group. So, you really may want to just get away from everyone, and be back on your own again. The soldiers stare at you as you know you have to make a choice. Do you want to go with the soldiers to find the king or do you want to slip away by yourself?

TO GO WITH THE SOLDIERS TO FIND THE KING, TURN TO PAGE 86

TO SLIP AWAY BY YOURSELF, TURN TO PAGE 149

GO WITH THE SOLDIERS

You decide to go with the soldiers to find the king. Suddenly, you hear the sound of footsteps in the distance! He is getting away!

"Guys, I hear him!" you yell in a panic.

The soldier next to you starts barking out orders, "You two, on the flank! You three in the middle!"

All of you rush at a lightning pace, catching up quickly to the king! Finally, you catch up to him and surround him!

The soldier next to you shouts, "Give it up, Zerx! You're surrounded!"

Suddenly, one of the soldiers bursts out, sword drawn, and deals a blow to Zerx! The soldier, next to you screams out in a panic, "Ronny, NOO!"

Zerx draws his sword and with two swift blows the soldier goes down. Under his evil breath, Zerx mutters, "Weaklings."

Within seconds, every soldier except the one next to you charges full strength at Zerx! But within that same minute, everyone who charged is destroyed.

All at once, you realize you are completely overpowered. You run as fast as you can, but Zerx catches up to you and hits you with his sword! You watch as your health bars deplete. But then the soldier standing next to you saves you, and knocks Zerx back!

"Fool!" Zerx shouts. You watch as your knight friend falls to the ground defeated! You realize that he just sacrificed his life for someone he just met. You make use of his sacrifice, and run as far and fast as you possibly can!!

You run and run until you have to jog because you are so winded. You job until you have to walk.

Then you see it: a huge village. Some might describe it as a mini-Tokyo. You notice a large pile of stuff on the side of the village road. A sign next to it reads, “FREE STUFF”. You think to yourself, “Wow, is this a Craigslist curb call?” as you wander over to it. You find a wooden pick axe with only a little bit of durability lost.

Proud with your new find, you decide to mine some stone for your house. You find a cave and start mining. You mine for a very long time and end up with about 2 stacks of stone. Your pick axe breaks immediately after you are finished. Then your stomach begins to rumble. You look at your hunger bars, and find that you only have 2 bars remaining.

Then you notice Mr. Cow wandering around the cave. As you look at the cow all you see is meat on a table. You pump your trusty fists, and go over to get the cow. As you do it, you think to yourself that Minecraft is so unrealistic. I mean, does McDonalds make their hamburgers by punching a cow to death? But who cares, you're hungry. You do the deed, and find it is your lucky day! The cow drops one piece of leather and two pieces of raw meat. You take the drops and go back to the outskirts of the village to build your home. You can't decide if you want to build a log cabin or a cobblestone house. You think about the two options, and weigh them heavily. Do you want to build a cobblestone house or a log cabin?

TO BUILD A COBBLESTONE HOUSE, TURN TO PAGE 103

TO BUILD A LOG CABIN, TURN TO PAGE 104

FARTHEST CHEST

You open the chest farthest from you, and there are 10 strength potions labeled, “The Gun Show”. You take them and put them in your inventory because you think they might come in handy later. But as you take them you realize you are standing on a trap door! SWOOSH! WHAM! The door opens and all in an instant you fall through a tube and feel like your fall will never end as your stomach feels like it is going through your throat and your knees tingle!

But then you see daylight! You go faster and faster until you land with a painful THUMP!! OUCH!! Three of your health bars vanish as you crash to the floor, look up and realize you are in what appears to be a big room where people come together in one area. Thankfully, there is nobody in the room, but suddenly you hear the sound of an army of stomping feet coming in the room! Then a man who looks like a leader comes in being carried by two big chunky guys. You realize you are on the stage where the leader sits. If he sees you right now, you are a dead man! You look around quickly for something to hide behind and quickly jump behind his throne!

The big chunky dudes place the leader on his throne, and each of them stand next to the throne while what appears to be the leader’s army stands at a distance on the other side of the room.

You breathe heavily hoping the big chunky dudes won’t notice. But. then it happens!

The leader cries out, “WHO IS THAT!?!?” as he points directly at you!! The big chunky dudes rush over and put their swords up to your neck and stare you down with a look of hate in their eyes! You know you do not stand a chance at battling because you are extremely outnumbered, so you hold your hands up in surrender and do what they order. They take you to the back of the room where there is an iron door and it to a hallway full of jail cells.

OH NO! They lead you to the end of the hall, open another iron door, put you against a wall and tell you to stand still. They throw a weakness potion at you and you instantly fall asleep.......

When you finally come to, you wake up to guards standing you up and taking you out of your cell.

TURN TO PAGE 17 "THE SOLDIERS"

GET ON THE MINECART

You get on the mine cart, expecting a slow and steady ride, but instead you get an extremely fast and bumpy ride! You keep going and going and going as walls of stone pass by in a blur! The mine cart tips over and you fall down into a glittery pit!!

You look around you to see that you have stumbled upon a mine shaft! But then you slap yourself because you have no pick axe! You suddenly see a chest marked, "Do not touch," and know what that means: "OPEN AS SOON AS POSSIBLE!!".

You open the chest to see stacks and stacks of pick axes, and in the center of the chest is a swiftness potion, a strength potion, and an enchanted book!

You guzzle down the swiftness and the strength potions like a man who just found water in the desert after walking without it for miles. But you save the enchanted book to enhance your powers when you really need it. Your muscles and your legs bulge up and you look like you just came out of the bubble bath.

But as soon as you start to mine the ores, an arrow hits you right on the shoulder and sticks painfully as you scream like a stuck pig! You look to see who was responsible for the painful arrow and in the distance behind a rock you see a dark shadowy figure wearing a dark hood and toting a quiver full of arrows!

The hooded person is guarded by two big chunky guys that look like the ones on the path to the cabin except they are ten times bigger than the ones you saw on the way to the cabin. As you look at the utter massiveness of the two guards, you feel like a dwarf from Lord of the Rings as you stand pitifully across from them. You realize if you're going to die, you might as well go down fighting.

So, you run at them as hard as you can, wielding your diamond sword, and swinging it sideways across the bodies of the two chunky guys and the hooded archer! The sword injures them badly enough to leave a scar for life, but you realize you will not be able to defeat them!

One of the chunky guys grabs your sword in one hand, throws it farther than the eye can see and with a mere flick of his giant pinky, knocks you clean out.....

When you come to, you realize your captors were intelligent because they made the cell out of obsidian, making it impossible to mine your way out. But then you think your captors may not have been as smart as you thought because you notice when you check your inventory, the only thing missing is the sword you used to injure them.

The cell has three small windows made of iron bars, a tiny bed, and a little vent that looks like it leads to the sewage pipe. You pier through one of the small windows, and get a shiver up your spine as you see more cells just like the one you are in, filled with other Minecraft builders who also have been captured. You look closely all around the cell for any possible escape routes. Two of the windows lead to the two adjoining cells, but one of the windows gives you a small glimmer of hope.

It appears that you have three choices. First, if you could somehow get through the iron bars, you should be able to get free! You would feel like an imperial storm trooper after just getting free of The Empire! Your second choice would be: the vent that apparently leads to the sewage pipe looks like a stinky possibility that would require a lot of wasted energy and a high tolerance for all things disgusting. And your third choice: there is always the possibility of sitting and waiting hopefully for something good to happen. Sometimes waiting things out works out best.

You weigh your options carefully as you decide between the three choices...

TO TRY TO ESCAPE THROUGH THE IRON BARS, TURN TO PAGE 93

TO TRY TO ESCAPE THROUGH THE VENT THAT MAY LEAD TO THE SEWAGE PIPE, TURN TO PAGE 98

TO STAY IN THE CELL AND HOPE FOR THE BEST, TURN TO PAGE 102

THE IRON BARS

You take your pick axe out of your inventory and slam it against the iron bars over and over and over again, thinking with every slam, *"I have no respect for these freaks who captured me."*

After several minutes of slamming the pick axe into the bars, they finally break!!!

You are so tired and sweaty from your efforts that you stop to catch your breath before getting up to squeeze through the window. As you stick your head through the window, you look down and realize you are on the third floor of the building. It is going to be a long, long way down if you decide to try to escape. You think very quickly to make your choice because you know that a guard could come check on your cell at any moment. Thoughts of freedom race through your head and you know there is no turning back. You squeeze through the window, positioning yourself to jump feet first. You let go and free fall out into nothing and it seems like it takes an hour to finally hit the ground!

As your feet hit first, you remember your Dad, Steve Sr.'s, stories of being a paratrooper in the Army and how he described landing when you parachute down to the ground. He talked about not locking your knees, and not trying to stand, but instead rolling with the force of the contact with the ground when your feet hit. As your feet make contact with the ground you instantly realize he forgot to tell you how much it hurt; but, you realize at the same time, he may have saved your life with his advice because you survive the fall.

Although you are badly shaken up and you lose half your health bars, you are able to get up to hear prisoners from the other cells yelling through their barred windows, "Hey bro!

Help me! Help!" You know you cannot help if you are going to survive, so you turn away from the building and run through the gates, only to come across the path of two night guards. OH NO! Your health is low, you are mentally drained, and now this just might be the end; but, on the bright side, they do seem sleepy, and clearly not expecting to have to actually do anything.

One of the soldiers makes a deep yawn, unaware that you are there. You take this opportunity to draw your sword, and charge at the guard, and strike him in the face with a slobber knocker! His helmet breaks and you hear the sound of metal crunching!

With a very satisfying knockout under your belt, you turn toward the second guard, and charge at him! Unfortunately, the element of surprise is not with you against this guard. He is already in a fighting stance. He draws his sword and you realize you are going to have to battle it out with this guy! He charges at you with his sword in front of him! You slam your sword against his shoulder, sending him flying into the gate! You think to yourself that you surprised that your sword has a lot of knock back power! You look at the poor guard and take pity on him because he looks like a little kid in the corner who got in trouble for bullying you. You revel in your victory until you realize you haven't won yet because he is getting up for more! He wasn't content with just being put in the corner, he now wants to go to the principal's office! As he runs at you again, you are happy to dole out more punishment! You jump at him and swipe right at his chest, sending him flying in a ball of ash and smoke right in the direction of the cell they had you in!! He disappears as he crashes his head into the wall of the palace!!

Exhausted, you hope this will be your last battle for a long time! You know that freedom is close to being yours, but at the same time your health is low; yet, you push yourself harder than you've ever pushed yourself before and struggle on, running toward freedom!! You continue to run, not really knowing where you are going!

Just as you are about to slow down from exhaustion, you see a black horse poke its head out from behind a tree at the edge of the forest.

There is also a chest laying near the horse. You walk straight to the chest, open it, and find a saddle. But, you think to yourself, *this all seems way too convenient.* This must be some kind of trap!

You look around to see a man with a toboggan on, a beard, and 6 pack abs. You instantly realize it is Zar, the worst griefer in all of Minecraft!!! *And you are about to try to take him down!!!!*

With quick reflexes, Zar pulls out his sword!!! All in one motion, he swings it right at you, and you do a Matrix move and dodge his sword! At the same time, you reach for your inventory and grab your sword, and aim it right for Zar's ! But, he knocks your sword right out of his hand by blocking your blow with his sword. But, you kick him in the stomach, and while he is buckled over in pain, you uppercut him to the face, sending him into a hole!!!!

You saddle up the horse, jump on quickly, and begin to ride away in victory!!!!

Man, you never thought riding a horse could be this fun! You are so excited to be riding instead of walking. You decide to name your horse Nelly, and begin talking to her like she is a person: "Nelly, how was your day today? Mine was really exciting. I escaped from jail, took out two guards on my way out of the jail, and knocked the world's most dangerous griefer into a hole!"

Nelly just looks at you like, "Would you please get off my back? It is really hot out here, and I'm tired." Just about the time Nelly gives you that look, you gaze up to see a group of sheep grazing in a field innocently. *Hmmmmm, looks like dinner time!*

You tell Nelly, "Wait right here while I go and get some dinner." But before you can get off the horse, she snorts loudly, raises her front feet off the ground, and bucks you so hard you go flying through the air, and crashing onto the ground in pain!!!

You have just enough breath to yell, "WOAH NELLY!" But as you look up, Nelly is sprinting out of sight and you realize you are there all alone and your health bars are almost gone. But, you have just enough energy to take down the lambs and eat them for dinner. You whip out your sword and give the lamb closest to you a darn good lashing with your sword. He yelps and runs away from you, but you chase him down and make mutton chops and wool for bedding out of him.

You decide to see if you can slaughter the other two faster than the first one. You're not sure which one you took out the fastest, but you know things are great when you get to take down three lambs and you're free! You are so happy to have some food in your inventory now!

Next, you take your pick axe, and start hiking, on the prowl for cobblestone. It is not very long before you notice a hill of cobblestone ahead of you. Oh my goodness, how your fortune has turned around for good! You are not sure if you should be thankful or surprised, but either way, you are relieved to know that tonight will be a night of rest and renewal.

You get to the cobblestone and mine and mine and mine because you can never have too much cobblestone. When you have 2 stacks of cobblestone in your inventory, you look at your hunger bars to find your energy is very low.

Time to whip out some mutton chops! You decide to get a piece of wood to create a crafting table. Then you put eight blocks of stone in the crafting grid, and create a furnace. Time to eat! As you finish up your mutton chops, you begin to think about your house you are going to build. There are a lot of trees around, which would make it easy to build a log cabin, but you also have plenty of cobblestone. Do you want to build a log cabin or a cobblestone house?

TO BUILD A COBBLESTONE HOUSE, TURN TO PAGE 103

TO BUILD A LOG CABIN, TURN TO PAGE 104

THE VENT

Before you go through the vent, you want to make sure that your plan is going to be worth it. So you go over to the vent, put your nose up to it, and take a big sniff. It smells worse than your Dad's toes after he runs five miles in socks and completes a year's worth of yard work. HORRIBLE! That is the only word for it! Yet, at the same time, in some strange, twisted way , it also smells like sweet freedom.

Taking a closer look at the metal vent cover, you see that it is screwed on tightly, and you know it is time to whip out your sword. So you whip it out and you whip it good!

You use the sword to pry out the screws in the vent cover as quietly as you can, but someone hears you, and yells, "What is that sound?!!" It is the guy in the cell next to you!

You try to quiet him, "SHHHH!" You realize that the genius in the cell next to you may have alerted a guard with his outburst, so you know you need to act quickly! There is no turning back as you finish prying the vent cover off, lifting it off, placing it to the side, and sticking your feet into the giant metal vent duct.

WEEEEEE! You slide down the vent shaft and it comes to mind that if Oscar the Grouch had a water slide, this vent shaft would be it, completely trashy smelling, nasty to touch, and horrible enough to make a goat want to puke. Your speed picks up as you travel down the shaft toward freedom! You are in total darkness until you suddenly see a light at the end of the shaft getting closer! As the light gets bigger, you begin to brace yourself for a landing, not sure what is going to happen next! You squeeze your body against the edges of the vent shaft to slow yourself down on your approach to the exit. As you arrive at the end of the vent shaft you hold yourself up against its edges so you won't fall as you kick the vent cover below you open!

The vent cover falls to the ground with a loud CLANG, and you hop down to a hard orange tile floor.

You realizc you are in the palace kitchen. OH MY GOODNESS! This is where they cook the food for prisoners, and it smells this horrible? You are glad you did not stick around to find out if freedom would find you in that cell! But at the same time, you know that it will not be long before you have to confront someone if you do not find a way to escape through this room.

So you sneak around quietly, looking for an escape route when you come upon a horrible smelling pile of slop with a sign above it that reads, "Cells 1-50". Oh my goodness! This slop is what the prisoners eat! It smells like rotten flesh mixed with toe cheese and chicken liver guts, and pig intestines mixed in. There is no telling what is in that stuff!

But then you look on the other side of the room to see a buffet of every kind of delicious food you could ever find in Minecraft. The sign above it says, "May the King, Queen, and guards rule forever".

Seeing your opportunity to get some good food in your belly, you eat as much as you can and keep the rest. With every swallow your health improves and so do your hunger bars. The satisfaction of knowing you are getting back at the enemy makes it taste all the sweeter.

But now to the important question: ***how in the world are you going to get out of here?***

You begin to snoop around and see that just outside the building there is a place for trucks to deliver the food. You also see a guy outside, sitting next to the door who is apparently waiting for a truck to arrive with food!

You whip out your sword and approach him like a cat stalks a mouse, and he never sees you coming as you turn him into a pile of ash and dust! It was like one of those action movies when a guy has to completely knock someone out to get their clothes.

You put his clothes on, sit in the chair, and wait for your freedom mobile to arrive. When it comes, you help the driver of the truck offload the food, debating to yourself whether you should punch him in the face or just keep helping him. You decide to go the sneaky route and help him. He goes into another room and you make a break for the truck!!!

You sprint toward the truck so fast that you feel like a sprinter at the Olympics, hop in, and slam the door all in the same motion!! You roll down the window as the delivery man comes out, and you yell, "Sorry sucker!!"

He yells back, "You can't do that!" He looks totally confused and extremely angry all at the same time.

You look at the floor board of the truck to find what may be the worker's defense weapon: a bow and arrow. You take the bow and arrow and shoot it right at the worker's hat. The worker looks confused wondering why you would aim for his hat, not realizing that later he will be in trouble with the king and queen for not having his uniform. They might even hang him. You peel out as fast as the truck can go, and leave the delivery worker in a fog of diesel fumes.

You drive and drive and know you are finally free!!! You have been through so much, it is hard for you to believe that you are finally free! You are not quite sure what to do with yourself. You see that you have only a little bit of gas left, so you begin to look for a place to build shelter. But it is a good thing you noticed you have just a little bit of gas left at this very moment because off to the left of the road you see a group of 3 sheep grazing on the green grass around them.

You pull the car over, hop out, and make your way to the sheep. You whip out your sword and harvest the lamb closest to you as you feel grateful for the food he will provide. He runs away from you, but you chase him down and make mutton chops and wool for bedding out of him. You decide to see if you can slaughter the other two faster than the first one. You're not sure which one you took out the fastest, but you know things are great when you get to take down three lambs and you're free!

Next on your list of things to get done for survival is to find and mine some cobblestone. You take your diamond pick axe, and start hiking, on the prowl for that stone that will keep you alive. It is not very long before you notice a hill of cobblestone ahead of you. Oh my goodness, how your fortune has turned around for good! You are not sure if you should be thankful or surprised, but either way, you are relieved to know that tonight will be a night of rest and renewal.

You get to the cobblestone and mine and mine and mine, because you can never have too much cobblestone. When you have 2 stacks of cobblestone in your inventory, you look at your hunger bars to find you have only ½ a chicken leg left. Time to whip out some mutton chops!

Thank goodness there are trees all around, because you are going to need to chop one down to make a crafting table. You take out one of your unused swords, and slam it against the tree over and over until you get enough wood to build the table. The harder you swing your sword, the hungrier you get.

You make your crafting table quickly, before you start dying of hunger. You craft the furnace, place it on the ground, put the mutton chops in, and a pile of wood to get this feast underway.

You take the mutton chops out of the furnace. Your mouth waters like a 6 month old baby's when you dangle a gummy bear in front of its mouth. You tear apart the mutton chops like a wild animal as your health bars go up. You feel very satisfied. Time to build shelter! You begin to think about what kind of shelter you want to build for yourself, and narrow it down to two choices: a log cabin or a cobblestone house.

TO BUILD A COBBLESTONE HOUSE, TURN TO PAGE 103

TO BUILD A LOG CABIN, TURN TO PAGE 104

STAY IN CELL

You decide to wait it out and stay in your cell. After all, trying to escape is rather risky. If you don't make it out and get recaptured, you might be done for.

As the day goes on you begin to doubt your decision to stay in the cell, but eventually two guards come, and start to take you away. You are really not sure what to think about it, and begin to fear the worst.

TURN TO PAGE 17, "THE SOLDIERS"

COBBLESTONE HOUSE

You decide to build a cobblestone house. Cobblestone will probably hold up better in the weather and will last longer.

You place blocks down tirelessly until you make the walls of the square shaped house. You then craft stone stairs to make a slanted stone roof on the house.

But there is one thing missing on this house: windows. I mean what's a house without windows? You decide to look for a small desert or a beach so you can make windows out of the sand there. I know it's called glass pane, but come on....they're windows for crying out loud!

You wander around looking for water so you can find a beach. But as you keep on going, you get so bored that you begin to think about the possibility of turning in a different direction completely so you can find a desert.

Wait! Suddenly you see water on the horizon! You know you are about to find the beach, that place where there is enough sand to build windows for the tallest buildings ever made in Minecraft!

As you approach the beach a creeper decides to give you a hug! BOOM! YOU DIED! **THE END**

LOG CABIN

Something about today just says, "Log cabin, log cabin, log cabin, log cabin, log cabin…"

You decide to go and cut down trees to make an axe in order to work smarter instead of harder. You cut until you have enough wood for your axe, build it, and start cutting trees down like the strongest lumberjack ever. You know you need 60 logs to make this log cabin happen, and you do not slow down until your 60 logs are in your inventory.

As you begin to decide where to build, a storm moves in above you, and it begins to rain. But you are determined to not let it slow you down.

But then you remember that mobs can spawn in the night. Your determined mindset turns into fear because you hear two *unmistakable noises: the sound of lightning hitting a creeper, turning it into a charged creeper, and the sound of skeleton bones rattling.*

An arrow hits you hard on the shoulder, throwing you into the dirt like a soccer player in pain after a brutal injury! You get back up weakly with your sword drawn! You see the skeleton hiding behind a tree! You lunge at it with your sword, but you miss!

Out of nowhere, a guy with blazing red hair and a blue sweatshirt comes out and shoots a deadly arrow right at the skeleton!

He helps you up by the hand and says to you, "Hey, my name is Michael. I see you are building a cabin. I am your new next door neighbor."

You realize he may have literally saved your life and thank him over and over again. Michael takes you to his house and gently takes the arrow out of your shoulder-well, as gently as you can take an arrow out of a shoulder anyway.

Then Michael says, "You need to rest." He puts you down in a bed, and puts himself down in a bed, and says, "Good night, neighbor."

You pray to God and thank Him for sending Michael, your guardian angel for the night, and fade off into a sweet dream about gummy bears and lamb chops.

The next day you wake up as your eyes adjust to Michael hovering over you.

Michael says, "I have two questions for you: 1. Who are you? 2. Do you want to be friends?"

You think to yourself that considering he saved your life, the second question was a bit weird.

You shout, "Of course, I want to be friends! You saved my life! My name is Steve."

Michael looks at you and asks, "Do you want to go to town with me? I need to pick up some supplies. We have the biggest village in the world."

Excited about going to a new place with a new friend, you quickly agree and you are on your way. When you get to the village, it looks more like Atlanta than a village. There are street lights everywhere, skyscrapers, and a wide variety of cars, all of them run by command blocks.

Michael asks, "Do you have anything to trade?"

You reply, "All I have is a few pick axes and swords."

Michael asks, "Do you have any food?"

Excited to let him know about your mutton chops, you tell him the story about the lambs you took down near the highway.

He says, "So you are the one who got my lambs!?" *Oh no,* you think to yourself: *here I am in the middle of a huge village with a man who saved my life and I brag to him about the lambs I killed the day before, and they turn out to be HIS LAMBS?*

Before you can beg forgiveness, Michael says, “It’s all right man. I have more lambs than I can count.”

You are not sure what caused your luck to turn around, but you are finding it hard to believe how awesome and positive a turn this journey has taken.

Michael says, “You can trade those mutton chops for ore over there,” as he points to The Man With the Yellow Hat. You are thinking to yourself that he seems like a nice guy who probably likes pets but is very quiet. You decide to stop monkeying around and get down to business as you approach The Man with The Yellow Hat.

The man says, “Hello, sir, may I help you?” Having never been here, you feel a little awkward but you know you can’t walk away without some ore. As Michael goes elsewhere to shop, he reminds you to buy emeralds because most villagers will trade them.

You tell The Man With The Yellow Hat, “I’d like to get 64 emeralds.”

He says, “That will cost you 23 pieces of food of your choice.”

You start to panic because you think you only have one mutton chop, but you check your inventory and realize that some buffet items will be paying for these precious emeralds.. You offer to pay the man with a golden apple.

His eyes sparkle in amazement, and he says, “Of course,” with his whole body perking up as if it were the best thing he has heard all day.

You complete the trade and begin to shop ‘til you drop. You have never seen a market like this one. There are lots of people trading and lots of things to trade. Your next stop is the blacksmith’s shop.

He says, “Hello, what weapon can I interest you in today?” You ask him for a set of diamond armor, something that has been shining at you in your mind's eye for a really, really long time. He brings out the armor, and it is everything you hoped it would be: a shining, gleaming shell of protection for battle that you have wanted for so long.

"It is 10 emeralds," says the blacksmith. Without hesitation, you hand him 10 emeralds from your inventory and take the diamond armor and put it on.

You turn to third person mode and check yourself out: you look AMAZING! You knew you would look good, but you look even better than you thought you would! And you're not vain at all.

You switch back to first person mode and ask the blacksmith where the library is. He points toward the bottom floor of a nearby skyscraper and you head that way, hoping you can enchant your armor.

You see Michael as you leave the area and tell him you'll see him soon back at the log cabin. Once you get to the library, you walk in and a beautiful villager greets you. She has hazelnut colored hair and a well decorated pink robe.

She greets you gently, "What kind of books are you interested in?"

"Enchanted books," you bark back a little too forcefully. "Oh do you want to buy an enchantment table or just have me enchant something?," she says sweetly.

Since you have absolutely no experience points to enchant your stuff, you decide to pay her to enchant some items for you. The sweet, beautiful, innocent looking lady turns into a savvy saleswoman all in an instant and begins to tell you all about the benefits of owning your own enchantment table: there's the fact that if you don't have the money one month, we can't take it away; there's the fact that enchanting is a lifestyle choice, not something you do once in a while; there's the fact that no matter how many creepers attack you, you really own your own enchantment table, it's really yours.....blah blah blah blah.......

Before you let her waste another breath of precious air, you interrupt and tell her, "I just want you to enchant some items for me."

There must have been something about the way you said it, because you notice that she freezes up all of a sudden and changes her voice back to the normal sweet voice she had at the beginning of the conversation, and says, "Okay. That sounds great! They cost 1 emerald for every item you want me to enchant."

You decide to be careful not to spend too much and only enchant 1 pick axe, 1 sword, and your diamond armor.

She takes a bottle o' Enchanting and pours it on to the enchanted book. Then she puts your weapons and armor on to the book and suddenly a small beam of light raises the items up and makes them glow. She hands the weapons to you and quickly writes a sloppy list of enchantments that were placed on your items.

You read the list. Next to the word helmet, it reads: "Blast Protection V". Next to the word chest plate, it reads: "Unbreaking V" Next to the leggings, it reads: "Fire Resistance V". Next to the word boots, it reads: "Jump Boost IV". Next to the word pick axe, it reads: "Smite III". Next to the word sword, it reads: "Sharpness VII".

Feeling great about getting your items enchanted, you are ready to leave, but you feel a strong sense of your mother being nearby as you feel a presence telling you "Read, Read, Read……Yes, Indeed." So you know the universe is telling you to get some books before you leave.

You walk over to some shelves and search around until you find two books that interest you: *Guide to the Nether,* and *Guide to the End.* You know these will be extremely helpful on your journey, so you feel great knowing that you were able to find them at the library. But you just cannot leave without getting more books. Your Mom would be so proud! You get one book entitled *Escape from the Stronghold*, and another entitled

Harry Crafter, a book about a Minecrafter who learns sorcery at a school called Log Warts. You bring the books to the counter for the librarian to check out, and leave the library with some entertainment in hand.

You decide to try out your jump boost. You turn to third person mode and jump as high as you can! When you jump it feels like you may never come down! You are amazed at the power of enchantment!

You decide to make three more stops, whether you need to or not. These emeralds are burning a hole in your pocket! You feel like a kid trapped in a candy store with 20 dollars in his pocket; you know the way out, but you just can't make yourself not spend.

You head to find a weaver so you can get some new clothes and pajamas. You open the door to see an old villager weaving on a stool. His voice is very soft and frail sounding. You can hardly hear him, but he says, "Hello. Can I help you?"

You ask him if you can have some clothes and pajamas. He quickly brings over an outfit and one pair of pajamas and says, "2 emeralds each, please."

You take a step back, extend your arms, and protest, "Hey, you can't rush fashion! I want to see what kinds of clothes and pajamas you have before I just jump in and buy them so quickly."

"Good point," he says sarcastically, "I don't understand this generation. This is the only pair of clothes and pajamas we have."

"Well then, I guess I'll take them," you say as you hand the man four emeralds.

He asks, "What color do you want them to be?"

You think to yourself that yellow would show up well when you are walking down the street, so you tell him you want the clothes in yellow. And you tell the man that you want the pajamas to have that sleepy little feeling, which only comes from having them dark blue.

You take the clothes and go to the next shop. It is a bakery where you are tempted by the smells of sweet and savory goodness all around you. The baker comes out and seems like he is having a sugar rush, exclaiming sharply and in an energetic voice, "What can I help you with?"

You hesitantly ask him for a few sweets, and he sharply replies, "What kind of sweets do you want?"

You say, "I'd like 7 cookies and 2 cakes."

"That will be 11 emeralds, please", the baker says with a grin. You hand him the emeralds and you vanish with your tempting treats of goodness in hand.

On your final stop, you go to the farm, and a farmer comes out saying, "Howdy partner! What kind of foods can I interest you in today?"

"I have been trying to get to this point in my shopping trip all day," you tell the man. "I am here for the best food God ever created: watermelon! The other foods are just details: pumpkins, beets, carrots, apples, bread, and potatoes. Also, do you have any red and blue wool?"

"Sure do as soon as I sheer those sheep over there, and I'll be glad to dye it."

You sit down and wait for what feels like an eternity until he finally comes back with everything you ordered, gives it all to you, and you pay him.

It's back to the log cabin for you! On your way back to the log cabin, you come up with the idea to have a friendship party for Michael and decide to invite some of his neighbors and friends.

You go back to your log cabin to set up the surprise party! You put up the blue and red wool all around the log cabin for decoration. You put the cookies and the cake in your kitchen for dessert. You make a self-serve buffet with all of the food you bought in the village. It all looks awesome!

You head on your way to go get Michael. You open the door to your log cabin. You see a boy with red headphones, a red and black shirt, and red and black pants, and blonde hair. You approach him to strike up a conversation; but, as you walk up to him, he draws his diamond sword and shivers in fear.

"Are you a bad guy?" he says fearfully.

"No," you say calmly.

He puts his sword away hesitantly, and says, "I was in the cell next to you. My name's Blake."

"Want to be friends?," you ask.

"Sure," you say, "Do you want to come to my friendship dinner tonight?"

He thinks for a minute and replies, "Sure. I have nothing else to do. I was born into a Minecraft world where people are only as busy as they want to be."

"Okay, great," you say, "I'm going to ask the other guest. And by the way my name is Steve. Do you want to come with me to get my friend, Michael? He is the one I am throwing the party for."

"Sure," says Blake, and the two of you walk to Michael's house.

You get to the door of Michael's house, and there is a doorman at the door. Blake high fives him and fist bumps him and says, "What's up, door man?"

"Do you know where Michael is?" you say to the doorman.

"No," the doorman replies, "But you can ask the butler."

The doorman opens the door for you and you walk in to see a beautiful house made of diamond, gold, and quartz. You immediately see the butler. He is bald with a mustache. You ask the butler where Michael is.

The butler says, "He is bouncing on his gigantic bed in the bedroom upstairs. Do you want to go up and see him?"

"Sure! Thanks," you reply, and go up to his bedroom with Blake walking behind you.

You open the door to see a rather odd sight: a rich man bouncing on his bed, with two body guards with sleek sunglasses on the bed, jumping next to him.

Suddenly, they stop jumping on the bed, draw their diamond swords, and hold them up to Blake's neck, yelling "Intruder!"

Blake looks terrified as the guards ask Michael, "What should we do with him?"

"Nothing guys! Look at him! He's terrified and he is with Steve, so he must be good!" says Michael.

"Sorry sir," the guards reply with a deep voice.

You begin to explain to Michael that you bought some things at the village that you want to show him, if he would be willing to come over to your log cabin for a while. Michael agrees, and you decide to invite his guards to come with you, so you introduce yourself and find out their names are Bartholemew and Brutus.

Blake, the guards, and Michael all walk with you back to the log cabin. You walk along enjoying the sunset, thinking about how great your life has become. It is hard to believe you have found a friend as good as Michael. You can hardly wait to show him your appreciation and are thinking about all the great things awaiting you guys at your log cabin as night falls on you.

But, all at once your thoughts are interrupted by the sound of zombies drooling!! With Blake's alert ears, he launches at the Zombie's without even thinking, and slices three in half! The guards, on the other hand, are picking off zombies with their bow and arrows! One zombie is stopped dead in his tracks with a head shot!

You and Michael whip out your diamond swords! One of the zombies comes at your head, but you have your new enchanted helmet on and you don't feel a thing, but instead lunge your sword into his belly button!

Michael has a Yoda style attack going on, jumping on one of the zombie's heads, letting the rest of the zombie's attack it and kill it. And then as the zombie falls, Michael swings his sword in a circle and kills the surrounding zombies.

With the battle finished, you all put your weapons away and walk to the cabin. It is completely silent, but you knew there will be lots of talking when you get inside.

Everyone starts bragging about their part in taking down the zombies. Once the bragging slows down, you get everyone's attention to give a little speech.

You begin your speech, "Michael, I told you I brought you here to show you some things I bought in the village, which is true; but, what I didn't tell you is that this is a surprise friendship party I am throwing in your honor because you have inspired me by saving my life and being a better friend than I have ever been to anyone. Thank you so much for your friendship! I can't thank you enough! Let me say a prayer and we will eat together and enjoy our new friendships."

You say a prayer and everyone gets their plates fixed and enjoy an incredible dinner with mutton chops, potatoes, bread, beets, apples, carrots, and pretty much every Minecraft food possible, including God's gift to man: watermelon!

Once everyone is finished, you say, "It's time for dessert everyone! We have a pumpkin pie, two cakes, and some cookies!"

The party continues through the night until everyone is completely stuffed and happy. What a night!

Everyone goes home except for Blake who you invite to stay in the cabin with you for the night. You craft beds out of the wool that the sheep provided and sleep in the most comfortable, deep sleep you have had in what seems like forever. You dream about being a world famous fighter with your new friends, and eventually going to a party with everyone in Minecraft.

You wake up in the morning at the exact same time as Blake. You both yawn like bears waking up from hibernation to the smell of smoke.

You immediately jump out of bed and look out the door to see the village in flames and villagers running from creepers and zombies!!!!

You and Blake sprint as fast as you can to Michael's house and pound on the door! Michael gets to the door quickly with his armor on, diamond sword in hand, and his guards behind him.

"Do you know what that smoke smell is?" asks Michael.

"Yes, it is an invasion!" you cry. "We need your help to stop it!"

Michael tells Bartholemew to assemble all of the other guards, tells the swordsmen to come with him, and orders all of the bowmen guards to the tops of skyscrapers in the village.

In a flurry of action to follow orders, there is organized chaos to prepare to fight!

You make a plan for you and Blake. You go to the village with Blake and the swordsmen, spread out through the village, and tell all the villagers to follow the swordsmen to Michael's house!

You come to a very shocking realization: some of the villagers have already been infected and have turned into zombies themselves!! You realize there is only one way to save them without killing them. You must take a healing potion from the alchemists' shop and use the golden apples already in your inventory to heal the infected villagers! You ask Blake to hold off the normal zombies for a while so you can grab the healing potions.

You hate to leave Blake to defend himself alone, but from the fight with the zombies last night, you know he is an extremely skilled swordsman. You run as fast as you can to the alchemist shop, fighting off a few zombies on the way!

You finally get to the alchemists' shop and grab all of the healing potions you can, and burst back out onto the village, which is full of zombies walking around drooling everywhere!

You throw the healing potion at the first zombie villager you see! Now you have just one minute to make the zombie eat the golden apple! You walk up closely to the zombie, your skin tingling with fear, and stick the golden apple in its mouth like a Mom giving a baby a bottle. The zombie turns back into a villager instantly-and not just any villager: it turns out to be the alchemist!

"Thank you! You saved me! Did you get the potions that were in the back of the store too?" she says.

"Oh my goodness! There were some in the back of the store too? I only saw the ones in the front of the store," you say.

"Come on, follow me," the alchemist says, and leads you to the store, and heads to the back where there are 25 more potions that will help you cure infected villagers. You thank her and tell her to follow the swordsmen to Michael's house.

You see two zombie villagers in the corner of the alchemists' shop and throw a healing potion at one of them, and you rush in to try to give it the golden apple, but the other zombie pushes you back! You throw a healing potion at him, and then feed the golden apples to both of them! You tell them to follow the swordsmen to Michael's house! You burst through the alchemists' shop door back into the village, and to your relief, most of the villagers are gone, hopefully to safety at Michael's house.

There are only four zombie villagers left, wandering around like hooligans. You decide to take a gamble and fling out four healing potions because you can see all four zombie villagers in your sights. Out of sheer luck, all of the potions hit their targets! You grab two golden apples and feed them to two of the zombies, then do the same to the other two zombies. You tell them to follow the swordsmen to Michael's house. You whip out the rest of your healing potions and go with Blake to finish the job by killing the rest of the zombies. You throw a healing potion, making a good hit on the arm of a zombie, and it drops and disappears.

Blake charges at a medium hoard of zombies, and turns them into chopped sushi fit for serving at a Chinese restaurant, but they would never pass the health code. There are 12 zombies left.

As you finish counting them, you realize you didn't count fast enough, and a zombie with outstretched arms attacks you, sending you summersaulting backwards! With your health in decline you realize this may be the way it all ends for you!

But when you stagger back to your feet, an arrow from above takes down your enemy zombie, and you are thankful for the bowmen! But another zombie charges you! But this time Blake is ready!! He slams his sword as hard as he can into the zombie and yells, "Stay off of my friend," and gains 4 experience level points.

You decide to drink one of the healing potions to get your strength back up. But as you look around, it seems like there are now more zombies than there were before you counted just 12 of them. You think to yourself that *someone must be spawning these nasty creatures.*

You know it is time to make a choice: either you are going to keep fighting where you are or you are going to try to find where the zombie spawner is.

TO KEEP FIGHTING WHERE YOU ARE, TURN TO PAGE 117

TO TRY TO FIND WHERE THE SPAWNER IS, TURN TO PAGE 122

KEEP FIGHTING

You decide to keep fighting! Blake slides like a soccer player coming in for a slide tackle with a sword drawn, and slams his sword against the legs of all the zombies. You come in behind Blake and finish off the group of zombies with your sword.

You think it is over, but once again there are more zombies coming at you that were not there just moments ago, and you know for sure now that they are spawning from somewhere. Blake tries to do the same move as before, but when he slides and hits the first zombie, the zombie picks Blake up and starts slamming him with his arms.

Now it is your turn to be the hero, you think to yourself! You charge as fast as you can at the zombie and do a flying karate kick with a ton of force behind it, and send the zombie flying into a different biome!

Blake weakly utters, “Thanks.” You give him a healing potion and tell him to gulp it down. Blake does it quicker than you expect him to, but not too soon because the three remaining zombies are on the attack!

You both pull out your bow and arrows and commence to firing away to hit and take down two of the zombies! You then follow up with your sword on taking down the third zombie. You look around waiting to see the next zombie, but the coast is clear.

You wait and wait, expecting for more zombies, until finally Blake says, “Do you think we should go and see who destroyed the spawner?”

“Sure,” you reply.

The two of you walk to try to find the source of evil that spawned all of these zombies. With swords drawn and ready, you walk cautiously. You walk and walk until you see two people. They both have gamer tags on. One of them reads, "Black Padawan," while the other reads, "Big Daddy."

Big Daddy seems like a really nice guy. With his red haired goatee beard and black hair, he reaches out his hand and says, "Hey, how's it going? My name is Big Daddy."

Black Padawan looks like a red haired kid who is very intelligent and likes wearing a hood. As he greets you and tells you his name, you and Blake introduce yourselves as well.

Big Daddy says, "We are the ones who deactivated the spawner. We are explorers and thought you needed some help. We'll be off on our journey now that everything is settled down."

You ask, "Do you know who spawned the zombies?"

Big Daddy replies, "Yes, we do. Black Padawan managed to destroy the zombies with his archery, intelligence, and swordsmanship. The spawner was a hooded figure. But he got away."

Black Padawan invites you to his house. You begin to walk with him and Big Daddy thinking about how grateful you are that you were saved. Blake follows after you, eager to see Black Padawan's house. You travel a long way until it is almost sunset.

In the distance, a minecart track slowly comes in to view. As you get closer, you find a chest, open it up, and find 3 minecarts. You place the minecarts on the rails, jump in, and prepare yourself for the ride of your life!

As you take off in the lead minecart, you see Big Daddy and Black Padawan riding at top speed on their own minecart right behind you. Blake follows last in his own minecart, screaming with joy! You ride for a short while, and feel like you are riding "The Great American Minecraft Machine" that you once rode at Six Flags over The Jungle Biome.

You all hop out of the minecarts and in front of you, you see something you wouldn't even describe as a house. It's more of a castle sized mansion! You open the door and find beautiful and ornate floors made of diamonds, emeralds, and some of the newest blocks in Minecraft. You feel your breath taken from you as you walk in and find a house fit for Kevin O'Leary.

You find a kitchen that has a sign reading, "Free Cake". You walk inside the kitchen to find two chests and a few furnaces. You open one of the chests and find enough food for an army. You find one stack of enchanted golden apples, one stack of normal golden apples, 29 carrots, a bowl of mushroom stew, 14 beet roots, 31 potatoes, 9 beet root seeds, 2 pieces of raw beef, 7 pieces of wheat, a stack of pork chops, and a stack of bread, one cake, one piece of leather, 14 seeds, and a spider's eye. Then you see is a big arm chair and a TV. There is a movie playing called, "The Noob's Revenge". Then you find a door that says, "Dining Room". There are purpur seats straight from the End. Black Padawan comes in after you heading toward his bedroom. In his bedroom, you find a chest, a light blue dyed bed, a crafting table with a flower pot on it, a chest, an enchantment table, an anvil, and a diamond sword on the wall. You follow him in to another bedroom.

Black Padawan says to you, "This is your bedroom." He turns to Blake and says, "Blake there's another bedroom that you can sleep in, and Big Daddy sleeps in this room," as he points to a neighboring room.

You realize how completely exhausted you are, and fall on to your bed. Then you are out like a light, dreaming about diamond swords and potions..

The next thing you know, you are awake in the exact same bedroom you fell asleep in.

You wake up to find a hustle and bustle in the dining room. You walk to the dining room, and find Big Daddy, Black Padawan, and Blake eating a breakfast of mutton chops and cookies.

You find that Blake and Black Padawan are talking some archery contest in another biome. “But, it’s not just archery,” says Black Padawan. “There’s a sword fighting contest, a demolition contest, and a building contest,” he continues.

“Sound like fun! We should go!” exclaims Blake.

“Ok, then we will,” says Black Padawan.”

Big Daddy replies, “You can go. But, I’m going to stay here for a little bit,”

“We’re going to train,” says Black Padawan as he pulls out his bow and arrow.

“Ok, I’ll come with you,” you reply. You follow after Black Padawan and Blake until you reach a small arena that looks to be used for training purposes.

“Here’s where we will practice our archery skills for the contest,” says Black Padawan.

“All right! Let’s do this! I’m pumped!” says Blake.

You, Blake, and Black Padawan walk into the arena, and find little targets with creeper heads. The three of you take out your bows and arrows and fire at the targets. Black Padawan hits the target right in the head. You hit the target right in his underarm. Blake fires and lands a shot right at the chest.

“Beautiful shots, Blake! Steve, you probably need to work on that!” says Black Padawan.

You think to yourself that you really are a lazy archer. You think about Robin Hood with a broken bow and tell yourself, “That’s me.”

“Perhaps you’ll be better at sword fighting,” says Black Padawan.

You and Black Padawan both pull out your swords. Black Padawan tells you that his sword is named “Sword of Evil’s Bane,” and that it is enchanted with Sharpness 5.

You think about the pain that you will feel if you get struck by the blade. “One, two, three, charge!” yells Black Padawan.

You do a classic Blake move, sliding under him, temporarily confusing Black Padawan, giving you the advantage. With his back turned, you charge at Black Padawan, but he turns around, sending you flying backwards into the arena wall. Pain shoots through your veins, and Black Padawan comes forward with another attack, finishing you off.

"Very impressive swordsmanship, Steve," says Black Padawan.

"Thank you," you say.

Blake says to you, "You're a great builder. So, maybe you could hold your own in the building contest."

Black Padawan adds, "And just for fun, on the way to the contest, we should practice our demolition skills by blowing up some Griefer Empire bases."

Suddenly you realize it! *You were fighting along with some of the most skilled Minecrafters in existence.*

The Griefer Empire will no longer raid villages, spawn zombies, or cause trouble for any Minecrafter ever again. You are tired of everything they have done to you and everyone else. You are going to beat them!!!!

TO BE CONTINUED IN BOOK TWO

FIND THE SPAWNER

Blake holds his sword tight, ready to cover you while you throw healing potions to try to get to where the spawner is! You throw healing potions on whatever comes anywhere close to you!

You finally reach what you think is the area where the spawner is. Then you see him: *a hooded man who looks angry and evil.*

He holds his enchanted sword like he is ready to knock you off the face of the Minecraft planet; but, Blake looks at him like he knows him.

Blake says, "Zerx! I haven't seen you since you turned against me and abandoned me to do the work of the evil! You had the strength to come to this place?"

You are a little confused because you don't know the whole story of how Blake and Zerx are enemies, but you know that something bad is about to happen. Your stomach knots up.

Suddenly Zerx pulls out a harming potion, and throws it extremely hard right at Blake, who falls to the ground! You run over to him to see if he is all right.

Blake gasps and says weakly to you, "Go on without me, do not let him win."

You whip out your healing potion as fast as you can and give it to Blake to heal him, and all in the same motion you take your sword from your inventory and slam it against Zerx! You remember how much knock back your sword has as Zerx falls 5 feet back from where you struck him!

But Zerx is ready to fight back! He takes out his bow and arrow and shoots you right in the arm! You struggle in pain to fight on, and thank goodness Blake comes to your rescue!

Blake uses his bow and arrows to knock Zerx back down and leave him down on the ground with only half a health bar; but, before Blake can finish Zerx off, Zerx steps on a pressure plate and you and Blake go falling in to darkness!!!!

You cannot see a thing other than black. You literally cannot see your hand right in front of your face! Luckily, you have torches in your inventory. You place them down for light but you can't see any better. You look up to see if you have any potion effects, and you see that you have blindness for 10 minutes. You feel around to see if you can find Blake. Unfortunately, Blake is not with you! Oh no! What happened? You realize you are all alone. You wait and wait in fear and hope.   Ten minutes later, you can finally see again! You never thought you would feel so great about just being able to see! You look around to see that you are in a stronghold.

You remember the book that you bought at the village and take it out of your inventory: "Guide to the End". You look at the table of contents, and you see there is a whole section about strongholds. It reads "Strongholds are the gates to The End. They are also sometimes used for secret meanings or bases for other Minecrafters. You stop reading the book because you hear the sounds of screams and people yelling, "Let me go!!"

You suddenly remember how the book said strongholds are also bases for other Minecrafters as you quickly jump behind the edge of a wall so you will not be seen and you can figure out where the yelling is coming from.

You peek out around the wall to see 4 people. One of them is a girl who has long cinnamon hair, and is wearing flip flops and a bumble bee patterned shirt. There is also a boy with wacky hair. He is wearing a black and purple sweatshirt, and yellow tennis shoes. The other two look like Michael's body guards except everything on them is red except for their face. The two of them are holding the boy and girl as prisoners.

You have to help them. What kind of person would you be if you just stood by while others suffered harm? You jump from your hiding spot and slam one of the guards against the wall, hoping to knock him out!

The other guard comes running at you like a neighborhood character from the old school arcade game "Paperboy"; but, you are ready for his attempts to take you out! You hold up your fist as he runs full speed at you, and he runs right into your fist and falls over, laid out, looking like he has little burglars circling his head! He is definitely seeing stars! You rescue the girl and the boy who both fall at your feet thanking you!

The girls says, "If it were not for you, we would be rotting in prison."

You say, "Well come on, let's get you out of here for good!" But you accidentally step on a pressure plate that sounds an alarm alerting a whole host of men in red suits! Oh no! You run and run, trying to find the path to a portal that will get you out of this place! The other 2 follow close behind you!

The kid with the wacky hair says, "I have been saving something special for this moment. He pulls out an explosive arrow from his inventory, and puts it in his bow, and fires it off right in the direction of the men in red suits! There is a BOOM so loud that you think you might lose your hearing! You see a cloud of smoke either coming from the death of the men in red suits or from the explosion or both.

You see the room with the portal in it! The girl takes out her bow and so do you because you see two men in red suits blocking your way. Pulling back your bow and aiming with precision both of you let go of your arrows at the same time and take down the two men!

The 3 of you rush forward to the portal and look back at the normal overworld and wonder if you will ever come back! The three of you jump in to the portal all at once and look up to see you are in The End!!!!

It is completely flat other than the ender pillars and the ender dragon. You have never fought the ender dragon but have heard many stories of people who fought him and lost.

You remember the only winning technique you have ever heard in the stories you have heard over the years and quickly order the boy and girl to take out their bow and arrows and aim for the crystals that the ender dragon feeds on to regain its health!! They aim like pros. The boy hits one of the crystals and it explodes.

"Bullseye!" he yells.

The girl hits a crystal on the edge. The crystal still blows up! She shouts and screams like a Baylor cheerleader!

There are only 2 left! You take out your bow and arrow and hit a crystal right at the bottom! It explodes! "YES!" you yell, but you know you are not victorious yet.

The boy uses an arrow to shoot right at the last crystal and pierces it! The explosion feels great because you know now that the ender dragon has nothing to heal its damage!

You yell at the boy and girl, "Fire at will! Take him down!" And the 3 of you fire away! The first 3 arrows strike the ender dragon so hard, but now the ender dragon is extremely mad!! He dives down at all of you and you and the girl dodge the blow, but the boy gets struck!! He is sent flying into the air and falls, crashing back to the ground.

"Oh NO!!!" shouts the girl. "Zac!! Get up!!" But an enderman teleports over and finishes off Zac for good. In a pile of ash and smoke, Zac disappears!

"No!! NO!!" the girl cries in anger. But she somehow manages to focus her anger toward the battle. "LET'S END THIS!!" she yells.

She takes out her bow and aims directly for the ender dragon's eye. She lets go and the arrow sails straight into its target! The ender dragon screams out in pain and flies wildly into the ground!! The ender dragon is knocked out but is not out for good!!

While the ender dragon is on the ground, you and the girl capitalize by attacking the dragon with your swords. But while you are hacking away in anger, the ender dragon gets up with only a sliver of health left!!

You both draw back arrows and put him out of his misery! He explodes in to a million pieces!!!!!! The End Portal spawns with a dragon egg on top of it. You jump into the portal and emerge in an icy biome to see 3 people standing in front of you in an ice cave. One of them is Zerx. One of them is Blake. And one of them is the long lost Zac!!

"Zac!!" cries the girl, as she runs toward him.

"No, Milly!" cries Zac, "It's a trick! Don't fall for it!"

But it is too late. As Milly gets close to Zac, obsidian walls come straight out of the ground, surrounding and trapping Milly, Zac, and Blake!!

Only your nemesis, Zerx, stands outside the obsidian walls. Your skin begins to crawl as you feel like your blood will soon boil from your anger inside of you!!

"Zerx, we trusted you," says Milly, "You used to be one of us!"

Zerx cracks an evil grin and laughs a dark and sly laugh and says, "You fools! You didn't see the winning side!"

At that moment a fuse in your mind blows. You can't hold back your anger any longer!!!!!! You lunge at Zerx and sparks fly as Zerx defends himself against your blow!!!!!!

"Get him, Steve!!" yells Blake. You use all of the strength you have in you to push Zerx back!!! Zerx loses ground to you, and loses his footing as you attack again, pushing with everything you have. Zerx is near the edge of the mountain now, and you reach down deep inside of yourself to give Zerx once last push...... off the ice mountain!!!!!

You look around to see if you can find any red stone signals to break so you can set your friends free.

"They're behind here," says Zac.

You climb over the small cage and take out your pick axe and break the red stone signal. The walls go down and all of your friends go free!!

You ask Milly how she knows Blake and Zerx. She tells you that they were in a crew together at one time and that they fought against the dark Empire as hard as they could at one time, until the dark Empire finally separated them, and they thought they would never be back together again. She tells you that Zerx was the one who turned on them and told the dark Empire the location of their base.

Now that you understand the parts of the story you were missing, you realize there is only one question that is most important at this moment, so you ask it: "How do we get back home? "

Blake says, "Our home is behind the trees in the distance," as he points toward a forest biome. You squint your eyes to just barely make out a few trees.

"Where do you live, Zac and Milly?" you ask. "We live here," they say in unison. They both point to a beautiful mansion made of ice, snow, stained glass, and nether rock.

"So if you don't mind, we are going to stay here," says Zac.

"Oh okay," you say, "Blake and I will be on our way back to our home."

Blake says, "It will be a long journey. Are you sure you want to go?" You begin to think to yourself that you are not really sure if you want to go.

You go over and sit down under a tree, looking very deep in thought. Blake comes over, puts his hand on your shoulder as Zac and Milly walk over behind him.

Blake says, "This is a big decision man! I know how you feel. I am feeling the same way. We have come so far and experienced so much, and yet our home is so far away."

"Let's just sit and rest our minds a little while before we decide," you say.

TO GO HOME, TURN TO PAGE 144

TO STAY WITH ZAC AND MILLY, TURN TO PAGE 128

STAY WITH ZAC AND MILLY

It is such a long way home that you are not even sure if you and Blake would be able to make it home alive. It would be a brutal trip. Not to mention that you would feel like you are leaving Milly and Zac behind, two new friends who happen to live in this gorgeous mansion you are standing next to. So you decide to stay with Milly and Zac.

When you tell Milly and Zac the news, they both hug you and Blake and are so happy that you decided to stay! Milly leads you, Zac, and Blake to the birch doors of the beautiful mansion, opens them, and you see a fountain flowing down like a waterfall, a quartz floor, a gigantic kitchen with walls made of prismera, and a TV that actually works.

"Well, this is the bottom floor," says Milly.

Your jaw hits the floor and you exclaim, "This is just the first floor?"

"Yup. We have an elevator to the next floor," says Milly. You find it hard to believe, but you follow Milly and Zac to the elevator, and go up to the second floor. The second floor is a huge bedroom with two huge beds, and a TV in front of each of them, and a chest stocked full of goodies.

"This is our room," says Zac.

Then Milly says, "You guys are going to like your room. It is on the next floor!"

You hop on the elevator, and when the door opens you can't believe your eyes! You are in a "guest room" that is almost as good as the master bedroom. There are 3 fresh and fluffy beds: one red bed and two sky blue beds. The walls are made of lapis and iron. The beds also have a TV and a chest full of goodies just like the master bedroom.

"Sweet! It's even my favorite color!" shouts Blake.

Milly explains that there are two more floors: the planning room, and the attic.

"Cool! I think I want to stay on this bed all day!" you say.

"I'm glad you like it!" says Milly.

There's something about Milly's personality that is just so diggable. She seems so content with the world, like she has no worries, and from the looks of this house, you think she probably has never had much to worry about; but, then you remember her story about being an outlaw, which makes her even cooler.

"We're working on building a pool on the ground level. Would you like to help us?" says Zac.

"Well, we have to repay you for these soft and fluffy beds don't we?" replies Blake.

"Then let's go down!" Milly says with a smile.

"Wait a minute," says Zac. "Why don't you come with me to get some supplies out of the attic, Steve? And Milly and Blake can meet us down at the ground level pool site."

"Sure thing," you say, feeling good that you will get to help out those who have helped you. You go up to the top floor on the elevator, and step out with Zac as he tells you to be cautious because the attic is dimly lit and mobs could spawn anywhere. Zac takes out his bow and arrow and you take out your enchanted diamond sword just to be on the safe side.

"The chest is right over there," says Zac as he points to a chest on the left side of the attic. You walk to it, but your fear gets stronger with every step until you finally reach the chest, and SMACK! An arrow hits you in the middle of your back!!

You look up to see Zac with his bow and arrow pointed towards you. "Hands UP, FREAK!" Zac yells.

"ZAC!?!?" you yell, "Why are you doing this?"

Zac looks at you with an evil look of determination and says, "Because I know the truth! The truth is that the members of the dark empire are the real heroes here!"

You yell back, "But you saw it personally, Zac! They are terrorists! They want to destroy us all! When Zerx is finished with you, he'll kill you!"

Zac whips out his sword, holds it in front of him like he is ready for battle, and replies quickly and confidently, "OH NO, he won't! Zerx has promised me a boat load of diamonds, emeralds, and every other ore you can think of!"

You close your eyes and open them again just to make sure this is not a bad dream. But, it is real: you are here all alone with a guy you thought was your friend, and now he has shot you with an arrow, has drawn his sword, and is telling you that you are his enemy.

But, suddenly you get it! Zac's behavior is not natural! The dark empire must be using some kind of mod to mind control him! You quickly look around Zac's body to see if you can find a device, but you don't see anything. Maybe you are wrong. The only thing you can do is get out your sword and defend yourself.

You try your best to talk sense into Zac as you hold your sword in a defensive stance in case he lunges at you. But Zac hears none of it. He only wants to take you out! He pulls his sword back to swing it at you as he steps, and when he does, you see your opportunity, and slice his leg!

Zac bends down holding his leg. You jump on top of him and your nose hits a head band on his head. You try to push off of him so you can stand up and fight, and when you push his head, a head band comes off his head and falls to the ground.

Zac stops fighting you and says, "What are we doing fighting like this? We are friends!"

All at once you know the head band is being used for mind control by Zerx, which means Zerx must be nearby.

Before you can say a word, an incredibly loud explosion blows a hole in the wall of the mansion, and Zerx bursts into the room!

"What are you doing here, Zerx?" yells Zac.

"Nothing," Zerx says rather oddly. But then he lunges at both of you with his sword! Zerx manages to knock both of you to the ground and destroy half of your health! Zac doesn't hesitate to slam his sword into Zerx's belly, knocking him to the ground!

As Zerx lays on the ground, Zac whips out his bow and arrow, shoots Zerx, and the knock back of the arrow sends Zerx flying off the ground! But he is caught by a monstrous machine that is as tall as the mansion and was used to blow the hole in the wall that Zerx entered to invade you. The giant machine looks like it is half way made from the killer robot's mod, and half way made from the entire supply of red stone in the whole over world.

"Do you like my new friend?," says Zerx.

"Uh, not very much," you say sarcastically.

"Well too bad," Zerx replies in a gruesome voice, "Because he likes you!" Zerx uses a wrecking ball attachment on the killer robot and begins singing a Miley Sirus song, "I came in like a wrecking ball!"

Into the mansion the wrecking ball swings and destroys the balls, one swing of the wrecking ball at a time until the outer walls of the attic are all destroyed!

Zac looks at you with anger and says sternly, "Well, if he is going to play dirty, then we have to play dirty too! That chest over there has everything we need!"

You summersault toward the chest and fling it open! Inside the chest are ender eyes and End Portal Frames, exactly what you need to summon tons of ender dragons! There are also five command blocks and one bacon block.

"We are going to use this to make that robot a pile of scrap metal," Zac tells you. "I'll summon the pig meteor, and you summon the ender dragon! And remember to place a command block and give instructions to the ender dragons through the command block!" Zac says.

You put the command block down and make the End

Portal, and put the ender eyes down to ignite it. Then out of the portal come five huge black and gray ender dragons! You put in the instructions for the ender dragons to attack Zerx's killer machine. The ender dragons go charging toward the killer robot!

"You think that'll work on us?!" yells Zerx, and sends out tazer arm attachments, shocking the ender dragons, but not destroying them.

Three of the ender dragons still have the strength to slam into the killer robot! As they slam into the killer robot, it endures 156 damage points for every ender dragon strike! But the problem is that the killer machine has 3563 health points. You look around for Zac because you know you are in trouble, but Zac is nowhere to be found! Almost all in the same moment, you realize Zac was a step ahead of you because now he is down on the ground at the feet of the giant killer robot placing the bacon block next to the robot!

And out of the sky comes probably one of the most hilarious and dangerous mods in Minecraft, the PIG METEOR, a pig face with fire all around it!!!! It lands on top of the giant robot, inflicting 245 points worth of damage, and then begins to fight back against the giant robot, doing 493 points worth of damage with every blow.

"Get out of here, PIGGY!" shouts Zerx as he uses a diamond axe attachment to hit the gigantic pig!

"OOOOOOOOOOOIIIIIIIIIIIIIIIIIIIIIIIIIIINNNNNNNNNNNNNNNNKKKKKKKKKKKKKK!!" yells the gigantic pig in pain! The pig uses its snout to make a gigantic gust of wind, which sends the evil robot back, enduring 644 fall damage points; but, the robot is regenerating quickly!

It gets up and uses an anvil attachment to drop on the pig's head, destroying it!

"Well, looks like it's pork chops for days now!" yells Zerx as the pig turns into ash, dust, and smoke and disappears leaving behind a gigantic pork chop!

Zac racks his mind to come up with something else that can bring down the robot. "Maybe I can spawn in the wither, and use command blocks to tell it to destroy the machine!" yells Zac. He spawns in the wither with soul sand and wither skulls! They spawn in like mob bombs and make a huge explosion as they burst onto the scene! Each explosion does 185 damage points to the robot! Then the withers shoot their explosive heads, each doing 74 damage points and putting the wither effect on the machine!

"You really are struggling with things to spawn, aren't you Zac?" says Zerx, as his robot grabs the withers and crunches them into oblivion.

"That did not go well!," Zac says with embarrassment.

"There's only one way we can do this!" you say. "I've only heard legends about it: the Batrra Larva!"

"Good thinking! I think we have a chest in here with its spawn egg!" yells Zac. "It's over there!"

You dive to it and use all the force in your body to open up the chest and grab the spawn eggs! You then throw all 9 of the Batrra Larva spawn eggs!

"We're going to take this thing down once and for all now!" you yell!

The Batrra Larva attacks the robot on all sides and it crashes to the ground with only one health point left! You and Zac throw yourselves through the hole in the wall and use your diamond swords to polish off the robot's last bar of health as Zerx jumps off, runs for his life and escapes, screaming like a baby!!! The robot makes a hissing sound and explodes, violently meeting its end!

You and Zac lay on the ground completely out of energy and breath, wondering how in the world all of that just happened. Really? A giant robot attacks us through a mansion? And we are able to kill it with pigs and dragons? As the two of you sit and recover from your exhausting battle, the thought eventually comes to you that you have not seen Milly or Blake since going to the attic. Oh no! Worry overtakes your mind and you begin to imagine the worst. Did they get taken out by Zerx before he got to you and Zac? Did they have to escape and you will never see them again? The questions and worries run faster and deeper through your mind until you finally say, "Zac! We have to find Blake and Milly!"

Zac says, "I was thinking the same thing! Let's go!" The two of you go to the front of the mansion where Milly and Blake were supposed to be working on the pool, but they were not there. In fact, there was no sign of them at all. Fear overcomes you and you look at Zac to see that he is just as afraid as you.

The two of you pick up your walking pace and start to yell, "Blake! Milly! Where are you?" You keep walking until you see two people wearing goggles approaching you. Not sure of who they are, you place your hand on your sword in case they try to attack you. Everything seems to be fine until they get right up on you and Zac, at which point both of them begin punching like a heavy weight champion at a title fight!

Zac takes out his sword and squares off with one of the goggled men while you square off with the second man. But the second goggled man is ready. He places a dispenser on the ground, loads it with arrows dabbed in weakness potion, puts red stone dust on the ground, and a lever next to the red stone dust. He pulls the lever and sends a weakness arrow right at your leg. You instantly start to feel sleepy and fall to the ground, sleeping like a baby. Zac gets distracted by you sleeping on the ground like a little baby and is caught off guard by the distraction long enough for an arrow to hit him and put him to sleep as well.

When you begin to wake up, your eyes open to see that you are in a cell....***AGAIN***....fortunately, this time you are not in the same cell as before; however, it is still a cell with a hard, cold, smelly floor.

Once you realize where you are, the first thought that comes to your mind is: where in the world are your friends?

You turn around and the answer to your question is in the cell with you. The four of you are reunited in a stinking, awful, hard, cold cell. You are so hungry, that every time you swallow, your stomach shouts, "Hooray!" You are not even sure how long it has been since you ate.

As the sun goes down on the horizon that you see through your cell window, you begin to talk with Blake, Milly, and Zac about how to escape. The best possibility is through the window. Every other possibility involves counting on your captors to make mistakes that will help you get out. As you discuss the specific ideas of escape, your conversation is interrupted sharply by the pounding of note blocks outside.

You rush over to the window to see what is going on and witness a group of about 20 natives dancing around a fire. In the center of the fire you see a strong and muscular man with a tank top with a happy emoji on it. What's this guy's deal, you wonder. You realize as you look closer that his hands are tied behind his back and he is about to be burned in the fire.

You turn around and yell to the other three: "They are burning the people they capture outside!" Just then your cell door opens and eight guards with goggles on quickly come in, slam the cell door behind them, and tell you to put your hands behind your back. You refuse to go down without a fight; but, in a matter of seconds you find yourself face down next to Milly.

As you look at the ground in front of you, the sounds of Zac and Blake yelling at the guards and escaping fill your ears!! You are able to see Blake and Zac knock two natives into their own fire before being captured by the guards!! There is a lot of screaming and yelling and guards cheering for you to be thrown into the fire. The natives line you up to meet your end. As they force you to walk closer and closer to the fire you resist; but, you know this will be the end. Or will it?

Out of the darkness, you see a large group of men with swords drawn for battle riding horses toward you!!! Suddenly, the natives are stunned except for what looks like the leader who is sitting on a throne made of hay. He barks out orders to the men wearing goggles to attack the intruders! The battle is on! When the men on horseback get close enough to see, you can't believe your eyes: IT IS LONG LOST MICHAEL leading the charge of 72 of his guards coming to your rescue!!! Wow!!! 72 of them, and on horses!!!

You think, *I wish I could get my hands free and have a bucket of buttered popcorn and a coke to drink while I watch this one!!!*

Michael gets off his horse and tells Bartholemew and Brutus to free you and the others. You wish you had been able to cross your fingers when wishing for the popcorn and coke, but your hands were bound too tightly. Bartholomew quickly comes to your rescue and as if he had read your mind, he says, "I can't get you any popcorn to sit back and watch this action packed one sided battle go down, but how about some cooked chicken, steak, or a baked potato a little later?"

Your stomach almost jumps through your throat as you salivate on his arm when he hugs you. "That sounds awesome! We have not eaten in days!"

"Come on!" Brutus yells, "I want to get this done!!" Brutus and Bartholemew jump full tilt into the battle with a vengeance, taking no prisoners along the way.

The battle is short lived because Michael's guards outnumbered the enemy so heavily. But as the enemy men lay on the ground, it is clear there is still one enemy to take out: the leader sitting on his throne.

All Michael's guards turn to the leader, and his eyes turn from scared to, "Oh my goodness, I'm about to die!" scared.

The leader hops off of his throne and runs in panic, yelling like a 10 year old girl who just saw a spider! He escapes down a narrow path!

The entire area is littered with goggled men, and it is time for you and Michael's men to cash in. You all walk around picking up food, goggles, weapons, armor, arrows, a strange little pig face called "Hiwatchi", and whatever else you can get your hungry little meat hooks on. What a post-party for the ages!

About the time you think you are finally finished picking up goodies, Blake points out that the natives had a bunch of tents, which probably have other supplies in them. Oh my goodness! It's a native flea market without any natives in it! It's time to get while the getting is good! You get to the tents in a hurry!

One of the tents reads, "Face paint and Head Dresses". You, Zac, Milly, and Blake decide to go in and have some fun! Blake grabs a head dress, puts it on and begins to dance around like a chicken with his head cut off!

"You gotta make it real," says Zac as he goes over to a purple and black head dress, and grabs a jar of black face paint. He puts both the head dress and the face paint on, making a funny imitation of the leader of the natives running like a big fat coward. "AHHHHHHH!!! My pants are on fire!" he yells as he runs around the teepee.

Milly goes over and grabs a bumble bee pattern head dress and pink face paint, and does her best impression of one of the natives telling her to put her hands behind her back, and her saying, "NO!"

You go over and grab a jar of sky blue face paint, and a blue head dress, and make an impression of one of the natives trying to make a house but continually falling over instead.

Michael enters the teepee to join in and grabs a red headdress and orange face paint. He does his best impersonation of the leader giving orders and says, "Actually don't follow me because my throne is made of hay!" You all walk out of the teepee, and decide to go check out the other teepees.

You walk over to a teepee marked. "Executioner". There is a chest that reads, "Ob Ze Ba Bow". You wonder to yourself what this means, and decide to open it. The chest is filled with stacks of emeralds and tons of axes with all the enchantments in Minecraft. You quickly swipe up the items and give them to your friends, distributing them evenly among them.

At the end of the camp there are two large teepees that read "Chief" and "Witchdoctor". You decide to steer clear of the witchdoctor teepee but since the Chief ran off, you decide to go snoop around in his teepee. You open the teepee door to see three cow carcasses hanging upside down! You almost jump out of your skin before jumping back out of the Chief's teepee. You think if the chief's teepee was that bad, then the witchdoctor's house may be safe. But you are not really sure of it. But somehow, curiosity is calling you over there.

You walk over to the witchdoctor teepee and enter hesitantly. You only enter about half way before you see the witchdoctor is in the teepee and he throws a poison potion on you! You get a slight glimpse of the witchdoctor as you exit the teepee. He has eyes that make his face look like death! They look like they are out of focus and looking off in the distance.

Chills go up your spine, and goose bumps stand up on your arms and your health goes down continuously until it reaches half a heart. You think the witch doctor is coming out of the teepee to finish you off, but at the last second, two people come to your rescue: one of their gamer tags reads, "Dr. Trayaurus", and the other gamer tag reads, "DanTDM"!

A surge of energy and excitement overcomes you and you are in awe that you are being rescued by two of your biggest heroes in the world! Dr. Trayaurus, wearing his white lab coat, snorts in villager language to the witchdoctor, who suddenly stops pouring potion on you. All you can figure is that Dr. Trayaurus knows the witchdoctor somehow.

DanTDM, in his awesome blue hair and cool black goggles stands over you wearing his iron golem cape. He helps you up and in his suave and charming British accent says, "Come on, mate!" He turns to Trayaurus and says, "Come on, Trayaurus! Let's go find the boys!"

DanTDM leads you to two people: one of them is named Thinknoodles, and the other one is named ThxCya. Thinknoodles has a cool gray beard and shaggy gray hair, and a sea blue outfit. ThxCya sports a dark green hood, and a dark green tunic.

"*How did this happen*?" you think to yourself. *One minute I was near death, and the next minute, I am rescued by my Youtube idols? This biome is crazy and wicked cool all at the same time.*

"Guys, let's go ahead and head to my house," says Michael. He continues, "Bartholemew, if you could kill a cow and make some meat for Steve, that would be great!"

Bartholemew follows instructions, takes out a nearby cow, and collects his reward of meat and leather. He places down a furnace and cooks the raw meat. He throws you your fast food, and you wish there was a McDonalds in Minecraft so you could get food even faster in the future. Oh wait, I heard about this mod that has McDonalds in it, but the burgers slow you down. I don't want that to happen. Hmm, maybe Chick-fil-A?

Anyway.....you are off on your journey and you have to catch up with the speedy Trayaurus. Thinknoodles and DanTDM are talking about tea and fidget spinners. Suddenly, you feel the urge to converse with your Youtube idols. You decide to go talk to Trayaurus about his latest experiment in the lab.

He tells you about a mutant ender dragon experiment where you place down a dragon egg and wait for lightning to strike. You are completely clueless on how in the name of science that would work. But, you keep encouraging him. You tell him about what it would be like to be a mod creator.

You think to yourself about all the possibilities of things you could create if you were a mod creator. Perhaps you could make a Pop Tart mod. There could be a golden Pop Tart, a regeneration Pop Tart, and a watermelon Pop Tart.

Suddenly, you are brought back to reality when you see it:

a glimpse of your old hometown, the big village you are so accustomed to being in.

You find a pile of stuff you never noticed before laying on the ground with a sign next to it that reads, "Free stuff". If there were flies in Minecraft, they would be laying eggs and spawning maggots all over it, a true sight to behold, while you hold your nose, of course. Maybe a Craigslister will come and pick it up in a few minutes? You think you see a broken wooden hoe taped together. But then you remind yourself that they would have to install some serious mods to get tape in Minecraft.

As you continue to walk, your gaze shifts back to the beautiful village for .5 seconds before it is rudely interrupted by Mr. Tree. "OUCH!" you holler. Trayaurus helps you up with a grunt that says, "You're an ignoramus."

As you approach the village, Michael's house finally comes into view, and you immediately notice that there is a whole new wing that has been added to the house. You think Michael might be housing DanTDM and the crew until they go on to their next adventure.

Suddenly, you see what could happen here: you could live with DanTDM and the crew until they go on their next adventure. You think about this idea for only a few brief milliseconds before you get so excited that you run toward Michael and burst out, "Can I stay with you?"

"Sure bro," says Michael. You feel like a puppy who just got adopted! You thank him about 5 times, and feel like you have won the lottery. Before you know it, you are right at the pathway to Michael's house. You walk up what looks to be a new cobblestone pathway. Every once in a while, you see a stone brick laying around instead of cobblestone. You think that makes it look cooler. You walk up to the doors and open the golden handle. You walk in and find that the wing for DanTDM and his crew is made entirely of diamonds.

Michael says, "Bartholomew, Brutus, build Steve a room.

He will be staying with us. And make it snappy! Thanks!"

They quickly respond, "Yes sir." You tell them, "Thanks." Your room is completed in just two hours. The diamond and emerald laden room is complete with a few bookshelves, a cauldron, an enchantment table, an anvil, a crafting table, and a chest. It's smart to be friends with the richest man in town.

You open the door to the rest of the mansion, and find that the person next to you is none other than the man himself, DanTDM. You decide to go over and see what he is doing, and find that he is playing on his phone from the iPhone mod.

"Wow, those cost a pretty emerald," you think to yourself. You ask DanTDM sheepishly if you can play on his iphone.

"Sure, mate," he says, and hands you the phone. "I just got a new game called Diamond Simulator. Just don't go into the creeper App, which blows things up."

You play Diamond Simulator, and find that it is actually pretty fun. The object of the game is to make yourself a diamond sword by getting to the crafting table in time. You think about how this game reminds you of a game you once played called "I Am Bread".

DanTDM tells you that there is a threat to Minecraft that they have just discovered called the Griefer Empire. DanTDM tells you that he wants to make a defense against it consisting of the strongest warriors in Minecraft.

The group will be called "The Diamond Republic". "The only members right now are me, the rest of the boys, and Michael. Steve, would you like to join?" DanTDM asks you.

You immediately say, "Of course I would!! I would love to send some Griefer Empire soldiers flying with you!"

DanTDM pulls a lever next to an iron trap door and tells you to jump in to the obstacle course! You jump into the hole and find that the obstacle course consists of ice parkour, a maze, and at the end, a mob fight. You are ready for this! If Michael could pass it, you could pass it with flying colors! You jump on to the ice parkour, careful not to slide. You jump and jump, and with ease you fall into the maze.

You think about how one of DanTDM's weaknesses is one of your strengths: mazes. You close your eyes and imagine the maze from a bird's eye view. All you have to do is go left, then right, then left, then right, then straight. You walk on and on, carrying out your plan in the maze until you notice something light green with a black sad face, also known as a creeper. You draw your diamond sword and are ready to fight!

Suddenly the creeper comes charging at you but you knock it back with your diamond sword! You run toward the creeper, strike it, and run back before it explodes. You do your last round of this and watch as the creeper fades away. You pick up the gun powder just because you can.

Then you see it right before your very eyes: the ENDING of the maze! You see light! You look up to find DanTDM dispensing mobs for you to fight!

You expertly end a zombie who is lumbering toward you! You see a skeleton hiding in the dark, trying to snipe you. You swing your sword and take him down. There are two cave spiders charging toward you, ready to bite and poison you! Behind them are two creepers! You take down the spiders as they disappear with a creepy crawly sound! The creepers charge toward you, but you hit both creepers with one stone! They fall to the ground defeated!

As if this weren't enough for DanTDM, you see the wither spawn right before your eyes. You take cover while you can, and watch as the wither powers up to explode. He explodes, leaving a gaping hole in the obstacle course! You take out your bow and fire rapidly at the wither! The wither makes its evil breathing sound in pain.

Then while it is distracted, you come in flying with your diamond sword drawn! You give one strike to each of its three heads. By this time, the wither is at half health, making him harder to defeat, and generating a shield that does not allow arrows to penetrate him. He shoots out a wither skull, sending him flying off of you! You feel the pain of the wither effect being inflicted upon you.

Suddenly, he spawns in four wither skeletons armed with stone swords. One of them tries to strike you with his sword, but you block it like a BOSS! You jump up, surprising the wither skeleton, giving you enough time to destroy him. But then the three others come at you! You knock all of them back with a multi-hit! While they are knocked back, you pick off two!

There is only one remaining! You dual it out with him. But before you can finish him off, the wither uses one of his newest attacks, which explodes nearly anything in its path! The attack sends the wither skeleton flying, destroying him. It does the same to you, but you manage to survive! You fall to the ground, but use every little bit of energy you have left in you as you grab your diamond sword ready to finish off the wither once and for all!

You jump up into the air, staying in the air for a little while. You manage to get off five critical hits on the wither. But the wither counterattacks with two wither skulls flying straight at you! You fall to the ground with only half a heart left.

"I can't give the wither effect any more time to kill me," you think to yourself. You hold your sword as tight as you can, very careful not to drop it. With your very last amounts of energy, you leap toward the wither, swing your sword at him, and destroy him!!! You fall to the ground, passed out.

The next thing you know you are lying on your bed next to DanTDM, water pouring on your face. "I did it," you mumble quietly.

"Yes, you did," says DanTDM. You find that your diamond chest plate and helmet are broken, and your diamond leggings and boots are badly damaged.

"You fought valiantly, just like a member of the Diamond Republic should," DanTDM says. He hands you a few golden apples, and you chomp them up eagerly. You sit up in your bed and think to yourself, “I am going to be fighting for one of the greatest causes ever alongside some of the greatest warriors ever. I’ll find Blake and Milly, and I will save Minecraft from the Griefer Empire!” **TO BE CONTINUED IN BOOK 2**

GO HOME

You decide to go home. You just love that big village with all of the friendly villagers, not to mention Michael lives there, and you miss him.

You say to Blake firmly, “Let’s go home. We have to make it home somehow.”

“That’s cool,” says Zac.

“Well then, see you around,” say Zac and Milly.

And with that, you and Blake trek into the snow. You walk and walk and walk until you come across a jungle biome right next to the snowy biome. Suddenly you see what you could do! You could make a snow golem!

You grab a pumpkin from the jungle biome and two blocks of snow from the snow biome. You put a torch and the pumpkin together to make a jack-o-lantern. Then you put the snow blocks two blocks high, and place the jack-o-lantern on top. Suddenly a snow golem appears! In a few seconds, you come up with a name for him: Eddie!!

You shout, “Blake, look at Eddie!”

“Aww, isn’t that cute!” says Blake.

“Come on! Let’s go on an adventure,” you say, and Eddie joins you.

Then you continue on your journey. You walk and walk until you find something moving swiftly, in and out of the trees. You draw your diamond sword out of instinct, and so does Blake.

Then you see what it is: three Griefer Empire soldiers ready for battle! You charge at the soldiers with your sword but one of them blocks it! Blake charges the soldier you were attacking and hits him like a Mack truck! The soldier falls to the ground in deep pain. You finish him off with a powerful blow while he is still on the ground. You use your expert swordsmanship to defeat one other soldier while Blake handles the last one. But as soon as you defeat the final soldier, you see just what you didn't want to see: three squadrons of the same soldiers ready to turn you into a grease spot! As if that were not enough, gradually coming into view, you see the man we all know and hate: Zerx!

Suddenly, Blake shouts at the top of his lungs, "You piece of noob!!" He throws himself at Zerx like he is turning from normal sonic to supersonic. He attacks Zerx, but immediately gets attacked by the soldiers. He picks off a few, but eventually realizes that he is outnumbered!

"Come on, Steve! We've got to run! We're not strong enough!" Blake yells.

Fear grips you as you yell at the top of your lungs, "Come on, Eddie!" You all high tail out of there as fast as your block legs will move! You say your prayers as you sprint as far and long as you can, wondering if you will survive. You run through the icy biome at top speed, but then you get an idea. You're going to have to get out of this the newbie way.

You tell Blake to dig a hole straight down. The three of you jump in the hole, and then cover it up with the snow block!

You sit quietly as you hear the feet of the soldiers stomping across the ground above you. You are scared but calm all at the same time, trying to make sure you don't breathe too loud. At one point, you think you hear a soldier breathing right next to the snow block you are under. In your mind you are thinking, *"Please don't let me die. Please don't let me die."* But then the soldier moves on, and you feel a sense of long awaited relief. Minutes pass slowly and you hear the soldiers moving away into the distance, their sound growing quieter and fading away.

Then the thought comes to you: *the Griefer Empire must be going for Zac and Milly.* Frantic, you start to mine out a staircase out of the hole!

You tell Blake and Eddie about your fear for Zac and Milly. Blake agrees, and the three of you rush out of the staircase!

You hide behind a small mound of snow and spy on the Griefer Empire, and begin to realize that your fear was correct. Milly and Zac are defending themselves against the Griefer Empire but are losing horribly! Oh no!

You, Blake, and Eddie have the advantage of surprise, so you hope and pray that is enough to give you an edge if you battle. But, battle you must. You know you cannot stand by to watch Milly and Zac meet their demise at the hands of the evil Empire. You and Blake and Eddie slowly creep toward the battlefield. When you're close enough to strike, you draw your sword and quickly fight for all that is good and against all that is evil!

Within seconds the Griefer Empire's numbers are lowered! There are only about ten soldiers, and Zerx left to defeat! Zac, Milly, Blake, and Eddie (who was rather useless) attack the remaining soldiers with a fierceness unmatched. The remaining soldiers are not formidable, but they are harder to put an end to than the others.

Your sword seems to glide with your hand, and clangs against one soldier's sword, then the other, then one of them falls. You fight on until only Zerx remains.

You see that Zac and Milly are very injured. But when they see the chance to destroy Zerx, they manage to regain enough energy and strength to battle on!

You run at Zerx, your sword ready to deal a blow, but Zerx pushes his sword in front of himself to block your blow, and winds up pushing you back after the block! You feel like a soccer ball getting cleared by a FIFA goal keeper who is rated a 99 on your PS3. You hit your head on the ground and pain instantly sends a shockwave through your brain.

You try to get up but you feel as if your friends can handle Zerx on their own. Then Blake charges full speed, but at the last second he slides at Zerx's legs and hits him hard with his sword! Zerx goes flying back, and Blake gives the signal to attack him while he is still in mid-air! He falls to the ground at Milly's feet, but being the varmint that he is, he gets up and runs as far and fast as he can!!!!

"That newbie little coward!" Zac yells. "He's probably going to lay down on his bed and cry about his newbieness," says Milly.

You all laugh about it, and then begin talking about your adventures. Milly tells you and Blake that she heard the Griefer Empire marching toward their door, and immediately alerted Zac. They came out with their swords drawn but were overpowered until you came along.

"You saved our lives, Steve! How could we ever thank you enough?" says Milly.

"A few golden apples would do," you respond.

"And I could go for some cake," says Blake.

You ask them, "Have you met Eddie?"

"No, we haven't. I'm sorry he can't come in the house. We don't want him getting snow on the floors."

"Okay, Eddie, you stay right here," you say. You walk into the house but find that you have to limp. But you make it to the front door. You open it and hold it for the rest of your friends. Milly leads you to the living room, and Zac grabs three golden apples for you and a cake for Blake. He also gets two golden carrots, one for himself and one for Milly. You chomp up the golden apples. When you're finished, you realize you have a massive regeneration buff, and watch as your health bars grow back to full health. Suddenly, your head stops throbbing with pain, and you feel like you could run 200 miles. Milly, Zac, and Blake all gain full health back as well, and you realize this massive victory deserves its own victory chant. It seems that your battle buddies were thinking the same thing. All at once, you all make eye contact, and without saying a word, it is like you know what the others are thinking.

You raise your swords high in the air and yell, "VICTORY!!! VICTORY!!! VICTORY!!!"

You know the Griefer Empire is not completely destroyed, and you will not stop until Minecraft is the same again, completely ridden of all Griefers; but at the same time, you know this moment is a new start with new friends, new enemies, and new allies!

TO BE CONTINUED IN BOOK 2

SLIP AWAY

Fear and hesitation get the best of you as you decide to more or less fake out the guys who saved you. You make a motion like you are going to go with them to find the king, and all of you go running in the direction he left. But you kind of hang back and let the crowd get ahead of you, and then make your move. You slip behind a tree and then turn the opposite direction around a corner that blocks you from being seen by anyone. You may not be the smartest Minecrafter alive, but the move you just made was pretty slick. You are right proud of yourself.

Now that you are free, you run for a very long time in one direction until you finally decide you need to build a shelter of some kind. You decide to either build a cobblestone house or a log cabin.

TO BUILD A COBBLESTONE HOUSE, TURN TO PAGE 103

TO BUILD A LOG CABIN, TURN TO PAGE 104

THANKS FOR PURCHASING THE FIRST BOOK IN THE PICK YOUR PATH SERIES!

Please take the time

to visit our website at

www.minecraftbooks.us

Visit the website to see:

- Youtube videos
- footage of the book creation process

- a video of Luke's own Minecraft world

- unboxing of Minecraft toys

- you will get a Free gift emailed to you

Plus, you will always be the first to know when a new book in the Series comes out!

Made in the USA
Middletown, DE
13 February 2020

84676730R00091